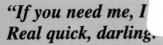

*"If you need me, I [...]
Real quick, darling.*

Shannon huffed in exasperation. "You'll do no such thing. I know how to dial 9-1-1 if I need help."

"I'm closer. If you'll keep making food like this, I'll come over every night and check your place for bogeymen."

"Ha-ha," she said.

Rory was ten times more attractive than any man she'd ever met. And a hundred times more dangerous to her heart. Shannon thought of his kisses. When he teased and called her "darling" she couldn't help but respond, even though she knew he didn't mean it as an endearment.

Life with him would be fun. If he loved her. If she loved him. She froze, overwhelmed at the idea.

Dear Reader,

It's the little things that mean so much. In fact, more than once, "little things" have fueled Myrna Temte's Special Edition novels. One of her miniseries evolved from a newspaper article her mother sent her. The idea for her first novel was inspired by something she'd heard a DJ say on her favorite country-western radio station. And Myrna Temte's nineteenth book, *Handprints,* also evolved in an interesting way. A friend received a special Mother's Day present—a picture of her little girl with finger-painted handprints and a sweet poem entitled "Handprints." Once the story was relayed to Myrna, the seed for another romance novel was planted. And the rest, as they say, is history....

There are plenty of special somethings this month. Bestselling author Joan Elliott Pickart delivers *Single with Twins,* the story of a photojournalist who travels the world in search of adventure, only to discover that *family* makes his life complete. In Lisa Jackson's *The McCaffertys: Matt,* the rugged rancher hero feels that law enforcement is no place for a lady—but soon finds himself making a plea for passion....

Don't miss Laurie Paige's *When I See Your Face,* in which a fiercely independent officer is forced to rely on others when she's temporarily blinded in the line of duty. Find out if there will be a *Match Made in Wyoming* in Patricia McLinn's novel, when the hero and heroine find themselves snowbound on a Wyoming ranch! And *The Child She Always Wanted* by Jennifer Mikels tells the touching tale of a baby on the doorstep bringing two people together for a love too great for either to deny.

Asking authors where they get their ideas often proves an impossible question. However, many ideas come from little things that surround us. See what's around you. And if you have an idea for a Special Edition novel, I'd love to hear from you. Enjoy!

Best,
Karen Taylor Richman, Senior Editor

Please address questions and book requests to:
Silhouette Reader Service
U.S.: 3010 Walden Ave., P.O. Box 1325, Buffalo, NY 14269
Canadian: P.O. Box 609, Fort Erie, Ont. L2A 5X3

When I See Your Face

Laurie Paige

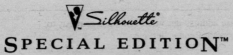

SPECIAL EDITION™

Published by Silhouette Books

America's Publisher of Contemporary Romance

This book is dedicated to Paul and Marci,
Steve and Andi with wishes for all the love
and happiness your hearts can hold.

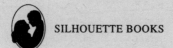 SILHOUETTE BOOKS

ISBN 0-373-24408-8

WHEN I SEE YOUR FACE

Copyright © 2001 by Olivia M. Hall

This edition published by arrangement with Harlequin Books S.A.

® and TM are trademarks of Harlequin Books S.A., used under license.
Trademarks indicated with ® are registered in the United States Patent
and Trademark Office, the Canadian Trade Marks Office and in other
countries.

Visit Silhouette at www.eHarlequin.com

Printed in U.S.A.

LAURIE PAIGE

says, "In the interest of authenticity, most writers will try anything...once." Along with her writing adventures, Laurie has been a NASA engineer, a past president of the Romance Writers of America (twice!), a mother and a grandmother (twice, also!). She was twice a Romance Writers of America RITA finalist for Best Traditional Romance and has won awards from *Romantic Times Magazine* for Best Silhouette Special Edition and Best Silhouette. Recently resettled in Northern California, Laurie is looking forward to whatever experiences her next novel will send her on.

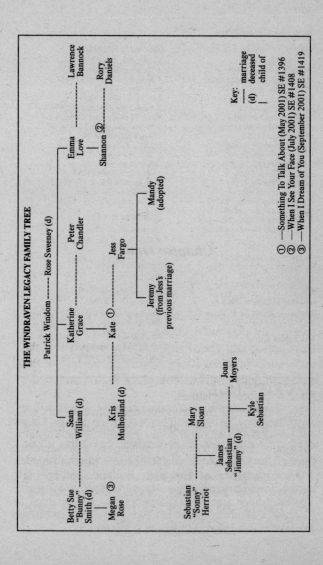

THE WINDRAVEN LEGACY FAMILY TREE

Patrick Windom ----- Rose Sweeney (d)

Betty Sue
"Bunny"
Smith (d) ----- Sean
William (d)

Megan ③
Rose

Kris
Mulholland (d)

Katherine
Grace ----- Peter
Chandler

Kate ①

Emma
Love ----- Lawrence
Bannock

Shannon ② ----- Rory
Daniels

Jess
Fargo

Jeremy
(from Jess's
previous marriage)

Mandy
(adopted)

Sebastian
"Sonny"
Herriot ----- Mary
Sloan

James
Sebastian
"Jimmy" (d) ----- Joan
Moyers

Kyle
Sebastian

Key:
----- marriage
(d) deceased
| child of

① — Something To Talk About (May 2001) SE #1396
② — When I See Your Face (July 2001) SE #1408
③ — When I Dream of You (September 2001) SE #1419

Chapter One

Shannon Bannock waved at the children on the gaily decorated float, part of the parade assembling in the parking lot diagonally across from her. Standing at the intersection, she directed traffic away from the main street of Wind River, Wyoming, where the Parade of Lights festival took place each year on the Sunday before Christmas.

As a detective for the combined police-sheriff offices of the town and county, she normally handled domestic matters for the department, but at this hectic time of the year, every officer filled in where needed.

Noting a group of kids and an adult approaching the corner, she quickly set out the wooden road barriers, then led the children and their caretaker across the street to a good spot to view the parade.

"Merry Christmas," she called to an old school chum's eight-year-old daughter as the festivities began. For a second she marveled at that fact—that one of her best friends from high school had a child that age. Next year would be the tenth reunion of the class. Amazing.

Of her old pals, she was the only one not married. Friends said she shepherded everyone else into family units but was afraid to try matrimony herself. That wasn't true at all. She just didn't wear her heart on her sleeve. In actual fact, she'd met someone she thought was quite nice, a new attorney in town—

"Yo, lady cop," a masculine baritone called.

Glancing over her shoulder, she gazed into light blue eyes and a face that—according to Marilee at the hair and nail shop—should have graced a monument as an example to all women of true male beauty. Rory Daniels, local heartthrob.

He was a respected veterinarian and someone she'd known all her life. He was five or six years older than she was, though, and, being an upperclassman, hadn't been part of her particular group of friends. Dressed in a down jacket that emphasized the color of his eyes, his hair blowing attractively across his forehead, she had to admit he was the best-looking man in the county.

The fact that he irritated her no end didn't lessen the impact. They had clashed over county land use, a street-improvement project and the use of woman police officers. He thought they should stay off the street and in the office. She thought women weren't utilized to their full potential.

In her opinion, he was opinionated and arrogant...in a charming way. She grinned at the thought. He was certainly a man to turn a woman's head. Some women, she corrected, not her. She had her life planned, and it didn't include a stop at Heartbreak Hotel because of a man.

"Any possibility I can get through?" he asked.

Seeing that the parade was at last getting underway, she shook her head. "Sorry. Unless it's an emergency?"

He stepped down from the pickup and stood beside her. "Not really. A mare being a bit slow about foaling. The family called and asked me to stop by."

"The parade will be over in twenty minutes," she told him. "Or you can drive down to the overpass on the highway."

"I'll wait."

She shrugged as he stuck his hands in his back pockets and stood with his legs in a wide stance like a man braced for the vagaries of life. When he smiled at some kids in the marching band that led off the parade, Shannon noted admiration in their eyes.

Actually, his name was frequently mentioned in the newspaper regarding seminars he gave at the local schools on caring for pets and livestock. He also helped the 4-H kids on their projects for the county fair.

Frowning, she admitted this didn't quite gibe with her image of him as an arrogant heartbreaker—

"Hey, Officer Bannock! Look at me! Look at me! I'm in the parade!"

Shannon grinned at the excited first-grader. When she called a greeting to a teacher, her breath appeared in long frosty plumes in front of her face.

Brrr, it was really cold tonight, below freezing according to the thermometer outside the drugstore on the corner. Storm clouds hung over the valley, capping the peaks around them. According to the weatherman, snow should be falling at this very moment. She stamped her feet and wiggled her cold toes in her boots.

"This is a night for warm slippers and hot chocolate," Rory said unexpectedly.

Nodding, she met his gaze. His eyes, with laugh lines at the corners, weren't arrogant at all. Instead, she saw something alluring...a speculative quality, an invitation to passion, mystery and forbidden pleasures.

Startled by this absurd fantasy, she nearly burst into laughter. Get real, she advised her heart, which had speeded up for some foolish reason. She turned sternly back to her duties. He truly was a handsome man, but so what? *Handsome is as handsome does,* as her aunt had once said.

Shannon knew that from firsthand experience. Her parents had divorced when she was ten. She and her mother had stayed in Wind River, close to their roots, while her father went off to find himself or something. For years, Shannon and he had only exchanged Christmas cards.

No, she definitely wasn't attracted to the too-handsome-for-their-own-good types. Home and hearth, a man and woman building a secure future for their children—those were the important things in life.

Shaking her head, she wondered what had driven her thoughts in this direction. The season, she admitted...and for some odd reason, the man standing quietly beside her, watching the parade with a tiny smile playing at the corners of his mouth.

A single person—even one as attractive as Rory Daniels, she realized—was sort of an outsider in the midst of all the family-focused events in town.

Waving at the Christmas Queen, she felt the loneliness dip all the way down to her freezing toes. Oh, well, it was just the holiday doldrums. Everyone had them at times.

Odd, but the thought of Brad Sennet, the attorney she'd been dating for the past month, didn't console her. Brad was smart, dedicated to his work and interesting. He didn't make her heart pound like in songs and love poems, but so what?

Friendship, steadfastness and respect—those were the qualities she wanted from a relationship, not a delirious loss of reason to passion, emotion...or a pretty face.

"How about that cup of hot chocolate?" the handsome vet asked, gesturing toward the café where Christmas lights beckoned merrily through the deepening twilight.

One of the teachers, another old school chum, overheard the invitation and waggled her eyebrows and clutched at her heart in a humorous display of awe.

Shannon suppressed a chuckle. An internal imp urged her to accept his offer. That would certainly set the gossip mill to turning in the small town. However, there was Brad to think of. She didn't play games with people.

"Thanks, but I'm still on duty," she told him.

"I'll take a rain check," he said equably and headed back to his truck. "Merry Christmas."

"Merry Christmas."

Curiosity caused her to watch him return to his pickup. Her heart actually thumped a little, which surprised her. That organ was certainly acting up tonight.

Mmm, maybe she had been hasty, turning down hot chocolate with the heartthrob of the county. Maybe this was one of those turning points in a person's destiny that, if allowed to slip away, was gone forever. Maybe the moment would have led to a great passion....

This time she did laugh. Come on, she chided her overactive imagination.

The fire engine went by, signaling the end of the parade. Shannon waved to the firefighters, removed the traffic barriers and stored them in the back of her four-wheel-drive SUV. Returning the barriers to the equipment garage, she mused on the encounter with Rory Daniels.

His eyes and that brilliant smile made a person feel special, as if his every thought was only for her. She wondered why she'd always considered him arrogant and distant. He hadn't seemed that way tonight.

Putting aside her musing, she finished some over-due reports, said good-night to the clerk on duty and headed for the five-thousand-acre family ranch where her grandfather and two cousins waited for her.

Checking the gauge, she realized she'd better stop for gas. It would be really stupid to get stuck out on a country road at nine-thirty at night, two days before Christmas. She pulled into the gas station-convenience market outside of town, then frowned in irritation that the ATM/credit card machine was out of order. She'd have to go inside and pay for the gas first. So much for technology.

Pulling her collar up around her chin to keep out the cold wind blowing down the valley from the Wind River mountains west of them, she lowered her head and headed for the store. Snowflakes began to fall all at once.

Great. Now the snow began—just when she had to drive five miles on an icy road.

She yanked open the door and exclaimed in exas-peration. Her glasses, a newly acquired nuisance, fogged over completely. She snatched them off with a gloved hand and headed for the counter, ATM card in hand.

At that moment, she realized two things: the man behind the counter looked terrified and the man in front of the counter was holding a gun on him. She reacted instinctively as the muzzle of the gun swung her way.

Ducking to one side, she dropped the ATM card and pulled the nine-millimeter semiautomatic from her holster.

"Police!" she snapped. "Hands up!"

The man uttered a curse.

In the next second—it was as if time had gone into slow motion—she saw the flash from the gun and realized he was shooting at her. Shooting at her! No one had ever shot at her in all her twenty-seven years. She was more outraged than frightened. Her police academy training kicked in and she took evasive action.

Darting behind a row of bread and pastries, she warned him a second time. "Put the gun down and your hands behind your head."

The man answered with another shot.

"Charley, get down!" Shannon yelled at the store owner. When he dived behind the counter, she had a clear view and squeezed the trigger.

The robber screamed as a red spot blossomed on his left shoulder. He spun away and slumped over the counter. The sudden silence was shocking.

Shannon cautiously stepped from behind the stacks of bread. "Drop the gun on the floor. Put your hands above your head. Don't turn around," she ordered, surprised at how calm she sounded, considering that her heart was going like a jackhammer. She'd never shot a man before.

The man slowly straightened.

"Watch it!" the owner shouted, his white face appearing beyond the cash register.

An explosion of light, white-hot and brilliant, blinded her. It seared through her head with a loud ringing noise that drowned all other sound. Through a strange rosy haze, she squeezed off another round. Her last thought was that she couldn't die. She had work to do, a future planned....

Rory Daniels clicked off the cell phone and muttered an expletive. His father and stepmother were coming to visit him sometime in January after spending Christmas with her mother in Phoenix.

Don't do me any favors, he'd felt like saying.

But of course he hadn't. As a dutiful son, he'd replied that he would look forward to seeing them. Ha.

His stepmother was a flirt and a social climber. The woman had tried to seduce him the summer he'd turned fourteen and grown to six feet in a spurt of maturation that had left him feeling gangly and confused. That had been eighteen years ago.

It had taken him a while to realize females of all ages were attracted to his looks, his money and his family name, one of the oldest in the county. None of which was *him,* the real person.

He'd learned to keep his distance during the years he'd had to dodge his stepmother and try not to hurt his father, who doted on the woman. College had been a relief in comparison to his home life.

But he'd learned another lesson while there.

After falling for a fellow student and thinking she felt the same, he'd realized she was concerned only with appearances when he heard her tell a friend that his black hair and blue eyes were a perfect foil for her blond hair and blue eyes, and that they were by far the best-looking couple on campus. With him as her escort, she'd be the Christmas Carnival Queen easily.

Her words had made him furious at the time. Now he only spared a cynical lift of an eyebrow over the episode and put both it and his stepmother out of his mind.

Yawning as fatigue and the warmth from the pickup's heater stole over him, he thought of a hot shower and a warm bed. He'd been through a difficult birth with a kid's pony for the past three hours.

The little mare had been too small for the size of the foal, but he'd managed to pull both through, the anxious but trusting eyes of the ten-year-old owner on him all the while. The girl had given him a strangling hug when he'd finished and pronounced both mare and foal well and safe.

If he could find a woman who would gaze at him in adoration for his skills or something besides looks, money and name, he'd marry her in an instant.

So far, at thirty-two, he hadn't run across that paragon. He knew what he wanted—a woman who was soft-spoken, smart and loyal, someone gentle and safe.

Safe? Now that was a weird thought.

Also, his wife would have to be a good mother. He wanted kids, at least two or three of 'em. Yeah, a librarian or teacher would do just fine.

A picture of Shannon Bannock came to mind—her smile as she led the children across the street, the way the kids in the parade had called to her. As a cop, she was sharp and competent. She was also headstrong, independent and argumentative. Not exactly the woman he had envisioned. So why had he invited her to the café?

An impulse born of illogical attraction.

The way she looked a man over as if judging his every thought and action was a challenge any red-blooded male would find hard to ignore. And she was built nicely, he added, amused by his thoughts.

Glancing at the gas gauge, he saw he had less than a quarter tank. Better fill up in case of an emergency over the holiday. Tomorrow was Christmas Eve. The whole county would close up at five so store owners could go home to their families. Nothing would be open on Christmas Day.

He wheeled into the gas station and stopped at a pump. Fishing his credit card out of his wallet, he noticed the Out-of-Order sign on the machine.

"Damn," he muttered and headed inside to pay. "What the hell?" were his next words as he stood inside the store.

It looked like a scene from a bad movie—bodies lying in pools of fake blood, an eerie silence over the place.

Only the blood wasn't fake. The salty, metallic scent of it filled his nostrils. It was real. And fresh. The smell of gunpowder hung in the air.

Putting his wallet away, he bent to examine the first figure on the floor.

Shannon Bannock, the cop he'd spoken to earlier at the parade, lay with a gun clutched in one hand, a pair of glasses in the other. She was on her stomach, her face to one side, her expression serene, as if she were merely napping for a moment.

Blood pooled under her head from a gunshot wound. He couldn't see any other injuries. She opened her eyes briefly as he examined her.

"I knew...you would come," she said cryptically, then gave a sound like a sigh and fainted again.

"Yeah," he agreed, checking her for other injuries.

He'd just bought a small acreage bordering the Windraven Ranch owned by Shannon's grandfather, which was probably where she was heading when she stopped at the gas station. Relieved that she wasn't dead, he quickly examined the other two and found them breathing. After calling 911, he retrieved his medical bag from the truck and began first aid on the three wounded people.

The police officer was the most serious. It looked as if a bullet had entered her temple, then exited under her lower jaw. He thought of what a bullet could do to a person's brain.

A few hours ago this same woman had been directing traffic, efficient and confident at her task. He wondered what her future was going to be now and experienced an odd stab of pain or pity or something under his breastbone. He looked out the plate-glass window. Where the hell was that ambulance?

Chapter Two

Shannon woke to complete darkness, totally disoriented. She put a hand up to her eyes and discovered bandages.

A hand caught hers. "Don't disturb the bandages," her cousin said.

"Kate?"

"Yes. Megan and I are here with you."

"What happened? Where am I?"

Speaking was difficult, as if she hadn't used her voice in a long time. It also hurt. She realized bandages were taped over her jaw and part of her neck, that they encircled her head and wrapped across her eyes.

Her eyes? Why were they covered?

Dizziness rolled over her, leaving her nauseated and frightened, a sensation that seemed all too familiar, although she couldn't recall ever experiencing it prior to this moment. Clutching Kate's hand, she realized she was terribly weak. And helpless.

"You're in the hospital. You were lucky. A surgeon from Denver was up at the ski resort with his family. He came to the hospital when he heard the news—"

"What news?" Nothing was making sense.

"That you were shot," Megan said from the other side of the bed. "Don't you remember?"

"No. Wait. Yes." Shannon paused and tried to see through the swirling fog in her brain. It even hurt to think. "I remember going in someplace and...yes, there was a guy with a gun. He shot at me. It really happened? It seems more like a nightmare than reality."

"You relived it over and over during your coma," Kate said in soothing tones.

"I've been in a coma?" This was becoming more bizarre by the minute.

There was a slight pause. Shannon imagined the other two cousins looking at each other and wondering how much to tell her. "How long?" she asked, needing to know everything, to understand what had happened to her.

"A week," Kate said, her voice soothing and firm as if she had everything under control. "The doctors put you in a coma to allow your body time to heal. You were very agitated after the...the incident."

Shannon tried to comprehend what the words meant, but it was hard to sort out. Struggling with an urge to fade back into the serene, foggy place she'd been for a week, she forced herself to concentrate. A scene popped into her mind. "The gas station," she said. "Did he get away?"

"Who?"

"The robber. I walked in on a robbery. I had to stop him. He was armed. He shot at me—oh!" Her hand went once more to the bandages. "He hit me?" she asked in a disbelieving voice. "In the head?"

"Shannon…"

The hesitancy in Kate's voice rasped across Shannon's nerves like a file. "What is it? What's wrong with me? Am I…am I…is it my eyes? Is something wrong with my eyes? Why are they bandaged?"

Kate gripped her hand again. "The bullet went through your temple, around the inside of your skull and out under your jaw. The bone wasn't shattered. You were lucky."

Lucky? Being shot in the head was lucky?

She almost laughed at the irony in that statement, but it hurt too much. She cautiously explored the gauze wrapping her head. "My eyes?"

"The doctors don't know," Megan said quickly. "One eye was affected, but the other—"

"Which one? Which eye?"

"The left one might be permanently injured. The bullet grazed it near the optic nerve."

"I can't lose my sight," she explained to them as

reasonably as she possibly could. "I have plans. My degree, the future, *everything.*"

There was the practice she intended to open when she got her Ph.D. in psychology. And what of her dream of helping families work through their problems?

"No," she protested, pulling at the covering over her eyes. "No. I've got to see. I've got to!"

She heard another voice in the room. "Keep her hands still," the new person said.

Little squeaky sounds accompanied the voice, as if the woman carried mice in her pockets. Shannon struggled with the hands that grasped hers.

"It'll be all right," she heard both her cousins say.

The words were a lie, meant only to soothe. "You don't understand," she told them. She was having trouble speaking, but she had to explain, to make them see...

Her mind went hazy. Sounds faded. She fought the darkness, then realized she'd been given a sedative.

"Don't," she said, her voice sounding far away. "I need to know, to find out... Oh, please, please, don't..."

She realized she was begging, just as she had when her father had packed and left. It hadn't done any good then, either. The tears came, helpless and despairing, then everything fell into darkness.

Shannon woke slowly, fighting her way through layer after layer of cloudy material. The room, which she somehow knew wasn't hers, smelled of antiseptic and flowers. An odd combination. She listened carefully, every nerve alert and tensed for trouble. However, the room felt empty.

The soft *clink* of metal against metal and the *whir* of a motor alarmed her, but then she recalled she was in the hospital. The floors were cleaned and polished during the wee hours of the morning. That was the sound she heard, coming from down the hall.

So it must be after midnight but before dawn.

She'd been dreaming—dark, restless dreams that still troubled her. In them, she faced the robber again and again, always experiencing the pain anew—quick, hot and blinding in its intensity.

Then someone—an ethereal being of coolness and light, such brilliant light she couldn't see his face—came to her, lifting her out of the hot pain and scary darkness, taking her to a secret haven, his arms strong, his embrace sweet, his scent fresh as the outdoors. She had instinctively known him. He was the one she'd been waiting for. He'd made her feel safe....

It was a foolish dream. No guardian angel had come to her rescue. An illusion, her mind's way of coping with the reality of being shot, was all it was.

Turning her head against the pillows, she gingerly examined the bandages covering her head and half her face. Pressing her left temple, she found that to be a sore spot. Also a place under her jaw.

It hurt to move her mouth, either to talk or eat. Swallowing the liquids they'd put her on was difficult. However, it wasn't as bad as yesterday, and to-morrow would be better than today.

Thus speaks the optimist, she mused, attempting a smile. That hurt, too.

That morning—no, this was a new day, so it was Tuesday, the first day of the New Year, she realized. The day before, when the nurse had come in, her mind had been clear for the first time as the heavy drugs left her body. Every sound had made a sharp impression.

During the day, she had listened to footsteps and tried to guess who the person was. She had known when Kate or Megan arrived before they spoke. And the hefty nurse who was always so cheerful. Her shoes made squeaky noises on the floor when she stopped or turned.

No mice in her pockets. Shannon had liked that image.

She had opened her Christmas presents yesterday, which seemed pointless, while her cousins described them to her. She'd pretended to be delighted so they wouldn't worry about her state of mind.

Still not quite able to believe what had happened, she'd tried to check her eyes during the night to make sure they were open, but she'd encountered the ban-dages. Maybe she'd hoped she was waking from a bad dream and that only the night was black, but it wasn't to be.

Everything was black to her. Day, night, it made no difference in her encapsulated world.

And never would.

Fear rolled over her in waves of nausea. She fought for control. The ophthalmologist called in on her case had been optimistic, but he had cautioned her that sometimes, when one eye was injured, the other, although medically okay, would sometimes act as if it, too, had been wounded.

Sympathetic ophthalmalia, it was called. There was a fifty-fifty possibility she would be blind, not just in the injured eye, but in both eyes.

Panic swept through her, pushing at her self-control like a log carried on a flash flood. She took deep breaths and willed it away.

The doctor had also said her right eye could be as good as ever. Or there could be a period of blindness, then the gradual regaining of her sight and that it could happen in both eyes.

So, there was nothing to fear but fear itself. Someone great had said that. President Roosevelt?

Relief eased the fear. She could remember things. People's names. Stuff she'd learned in school. Incidents from the past. She'd pestered Megan and Kate on their visits, making them test her so that she would know her mind was functioning normally.

A mind is a terrible thing to lose.

A slogan for an anti-drug campaign, she recalled. They didn't know the half of it. Brain damage. It was a thought that frightened her even more than blindness. However, her mind appeared okay.

It had been a week and two days since the shoot-out. If she really did lose her sight... She tried to imagine it, to see herself coping, tapping her way through life with a white cane. The blackness seemed to darken more. She would be a burden, dependent on others the rest of her life.

But it was too early to think like that, the doctor had assured her. There was a chance. Fifty-fifty. Not bad odds for a person who'd been shot in the head.

Tears filled her eyes and spilled into the bandages. She willed them away. Crying did no good whatsoever.

Hearing a man's voice in the hall, she wondered where Brad was. He hadn't visited, or even called.

What man in his right mind would tie himself to someone who might be blind for life? a cynical part of her asked.

The man who loved her, came the answer from her never-say-die counterpart.

A hopeless romantic, she had always believed a couple could make it through any tragedy, but it took strength and dedication from both of them. If she and Brad had married, would they have made it through this crisis?

Maybe. *If he had loved her. If she had loved him.*

Love was the key. She had thought that was a possibility with Brad, but now...

The expectation faded into mist, like dreams barely recalled when dawn came. She felt the loss deep within, a nostalgia for what might have been, rather than what actually was. She had longed for a great love. Without it, life would be lonely.

Inhaling carefully, as if the slightest movement

might cause her to shatter, she thought of her guardian angel, the one who had comforted her and eased the fear with his cool touch. He hadn't been real, but that didn't stop her from clinging to the memory or the dream of him or whatever it had been. Maybe she would meet a man like that.

Riding that small raft of comfort in the troubled sea of darkness that was now her future, she drifted toward sleep once more.

Rory stood outside the door of room 212. He glanced at the pot of poinsettias he'd brought. They seemed pointless now, after he'd spoken with Shannon's cousin in the parking lot. Shannon wouldn't be able to see them. Both her eyes were bandaged. The doctors didn't know the outcome yet. She might be blind.

He pictured her in her police uniform, swinging across the street with a bouncy step. Her hat had sat at a jaunty angle on her head, and she'd been leading a group of children across the street. The Pied Piper of Wind River, he'd thought in amusement at the time. The later picture, the one of her shot and bleeding, didn't seem real.

A funny ache tapped behind his sternum as he went into the room. He wasn't, he saw, the only one who'd thought of flowers. Vases and baskets of them covered nearly every surface and overflowed onto the floor, filling the corners of the room with lush color that reminded him of spring.

The patient was asleep.

He set the flowerpot on the windowsill, then stood beside the bed and studied her face. Beneath the massive bandages covering her head like a turban, he could see bruises along her left cheek. The rest of her face was pale.

Except for her lips. They were pink and full.

Her mouth wasn't wide, but it had an appeal that made a man want to lean forward and experience for himself the taste of those dewy lips. For some reason he'd wanted to do the same thing at the parade that night.

Frowning, he drew back. He'd seen his share of attractive women... But there was something very appealing about this particular female—when she wasn't arguing the opposite side of an issue with him. Maybe it was because she was asleep. A man just naturally wanted to wake her with a kiss.

Cynically amused at his own thoughts—Prince Charming he wasn't—he stepped back from the bed and took in the whole array of medical equipment. The lady cop had been seriously wounded. If he'd been seconds later in arriving, the outcome could have been much different.

It certainly seemed to be an odd case, still of interest to the local news media, although the story hadn't made it to national broadcasts.

The other two victims had been released from the hospital. The store owner couldn't remember anything about the incident. The customer couldn't identify the robber, who, he said, wore surgical gloves and a stocking over his face. Walking in on the robbery, he had struggled over a gun after the crook had shot the officer and the store owner and gotten himself shot as a reward for his efforts.

No gun or identifiable fingerprints had been found at the crime scene. There had been no trace of the perpetrator at the shoot-out, as the media had dubbed the incident due to the number of shots fired. Six in all, four from the robber's gun, two from Shannon's. If she ended up blind, then she wouldn't be able to identify the perp, either, assuming the cops ever found the guy.

Rory didn't know how much of the story was true. All his information came from the local paper.

He paused in his ruminations when Shannon shifted restlessly. Her lips moved in a murmur. Although his practice didn't extend to the human animal, he checked her pulse anyway. It was fast. When she became more and more agitated in the grip of her nightmare, he debated ringing for the nurse and asking about a sedative.

As he hesitated, the sun emerged from a cloud. Its rays, streaming in through the window, caught in the strands of hair across the pillow. Fascinated, he stared at the luxuriant tangles. Her hair flowed from under the white gauze in long, curly tendrils. Where the sunlight hit it, the strands glinted in shades of tawny blond and auburn, like darkly burnished gold, a secret treasure waiting to be discovered.

He lifted a curl and watched it curve over his finger and cling, as if it had a mind of its own.

''Beautiful, isn't it? And the color is natural. You

can tell by the roots." A nurse came in and checked various things—the patient's vital signs, the level of water in a pitcher on the bedside stand. "Miss Bannock? How do you feel today? You want to sit up?"

Rory stepped back to give the nurse some space. He saw Shannon's head turn toward the woman's voice and tried to recall the color of her eyes. He noticed the smallness of her hand resting on the sheet.

She was on the slender side, but tall, probably five-eight, like her cousin, Kate, who had been a grade ahead of him in school from the time he started kindergarten until they'd graduated from the same state university a year apart.

He'd had a terrible crush on the "older" woman in high school, something she'd never known. After college, he'd gone on to vet school and Kate had married someone else.

"You have company today, someone other than your cousins and the sheriff and detectives," the nurse reported to the patient in tones too cheerful to be real as she went to the other side of the bed, smoothing the covers as she did. "A handsome young man." She cast him a playful glance.

"Hi," he said, stepping up to the bed again. His voice came out as falsely cheerful as the nurse's. He cleared it self-consciously. "How're you feeling?"

Now that was a brilliant question to ask someone who'd been shot in the head. Disgusted, he tried to think of something to add, but his mind went blank. So much for social skills.

"Fine," she said politely. "Uh, do you mind telling me who you are? I'm not good with voices yet. Except for Kate and Megan.''

"Rory Daniels. Sorry, I should have mentioned it.''

"That's okay. Rory,'' she repeated as if testing the name against some memory.

For a second, she seemed disappointed, then she smiled. Her lips tipped up at the corners and dimples appeared in her cheeks. Even with that just-begging-for-a-kiss mouth, the dimples made her look young and vulnerable beneath the pile of bandages.

"How nice of you to stop by,'' she continued in a polite manner that set his teeth on edge. "Oh, and Happy New Year.''

As if they were at a tea party or some damn thing. It made his chest ache in that odd way.

The nurse pushed a button and the bed slowly rose, bringing the patient to a full sitting position.

When the bed stopped, Shannon turned toward him as if she could see. "It seems I have you to thank for saving my life. The paramedic said you called for help, then controlled the bleeding until they arrived. A very good Samaritan indeed.''

She stopped speaking. The alluring smile disappeared. The soft-looking lips trembled, then firmed as she smiled once more. He added self-control to her list of attributes.

"It was nothing. Don't think about it if the memory bothers you,'' he quickly said.

"No, I want to remember. Would you help by telling me everything you saw?''

He mulled over the scene at the mini-mart while

the nurse brought a robe from the closet, deftly slipped it on the patient, then bent to put on slippers. "Why don't you escort her down to the sunroom? The patient is tired of these four walls," she said without checking with Shannon.

"Sure."

Rory took hold of Shannon's arm and steadied her as she got out of bed. The nurse, beaming with good-will, saw them on their way, then bustled about straightening the room, her shoes making curious little noises on the tiles.

"This is the first time I've been out of the room since I got here. I'm sort of nervous," Shannon admitted as they walked slowly down the broad corridor.

"So am I."

"You? Why?"

"I want to kiss you."

She stopped abruptly. Her head whipped around toward him, then she groaned and put a hand to her temple.

"Sorry," he murmured, resisting an urge to put his arm around her waist and pull her closer. "I didn't mean to startle you. I should have guarded my tongue."

The smile fluttered over her lips. "Well, now that you have my attention, what did you really want to say?"

He laughed, relieved at her humor and sassiness. "Here we are. Turn right," he directed.

They went into the pleasant, window-lined room.

The winter sun played hide-and-seek through a thin covering of clouds. "Do you recall what the room looks like?" he asked.

"Not really. Windows and plants, I think."

He described the potted trees and plants, the way the snow lay upon the rolling grounds of the hospital and on the peaks outlining the sky, the gleam of the sun shining on the red Mexican tiles.

"I brought you a poinsettia," he added. "You have about a thousand baskets of flowers in your room. We should have brought some down here."

"Good idea. I'll tell the nurse." She took a seat in the cane-backed rocker he directed her toward. "Now. Tell me what you saw when you went in the gas station. First, what kind of vehicles were outside?"

"That's what Kate's husband asked," Rory told her. "He wanted every detail I could recall."

Kate's first marriage had ended in tragedy a few years ago. She'd recently married a cop. The man had a son, and the couple was adopting a little girl. When he saw them in town, they were the picture of a happy family.

For an instant, he felt the strangest emotion, then realized what it was—envy.

Not that he was still mooning over Kate, but sometimes a man felt the emptiness in his life. Like at Christmas.

Shannon nodded. "Jess is in charge of investigations for the department. He's grilled me, too. Between him and the sheriff, I began to wonder if I had robbed the place and shot myself to cover up the crime.''

He chuckled at her wry grimace, which caused the dimples to flash in and out. ''Let's see, there was your SUV at the gas pump in front of my truck,'' Rory said, picturing the gas station, its lights hazy in the falling snow. ''A pickup was parked at the side of the building, where the air and water hoses are located. I think there was another one at the curb near the door. That was all I saw.''

''You didn't see anyone driving off when you arrived?''

''No.''

''You didn't notice any fresh tire tracks in the snow where someone might have just driven off?''

''No, sorry. Clues to a crime weren't on my mind at the moment. I was thinking of home and bed. I didn't notice anything until I walked in the store and saw three bodies lying on the floor.''

''I told the sheriff there wasn't anyone else. The perp had to be the other man in the store.'' She sighed and raised a hand to her bandaged temple. ''No one believes me.''

Rory sensed her frustration. Lacking evidence, since the store owner didn't remember anything at all, the sheriff had let the other man go when he was released from the hospital with only a slight flesh wound from the shooting. Without sight, Shannon couldn't identify the man, even if he was the guilty party.

Eyeing the thick bandages, Rory considered her future. Being blinded in the line of duty was a hell of a way to end a police career. He wondered what she would do now.

"Take me back to my room, please," she said suddenly, standing, her hands trembling as she reached out to him.

He wondered guiltily if she had somehow read his thoughts concerning her future. He took her arm and led her back the way they had come. Her cousin Kate was waiting for them. Seeing her reminded him of another reason for his visit. He removed an ATM card from his jacket pocket and handed it to Kate, along with a pair of glasses.

"The card was on the floor. I found the glasses in her hand," he explained.

Kate gave him a hug for saving her "second favorite" cousin. Her smile was conspiratorial.

"Hey, I thought I was the favorite and Megan was second," Shannon protested.

The lighthearted tone surprised him. Studying the lady cop and her smile, which looked rather comical, coming as it did from a head swathed with bandages, Rory felt that odd pang in his chest again. She was scrappy, this one.

Glancing at his watch, he saw it was time for him to report back to the office. "Duty calls," he told the women. "Good to see you again, Kate. Take care, lady cop."

He smiled for Kate and looked Shannon over once more, finding it hard to reconcile the confident, buoyant officer who'd held the world in her hands with

the woman whose hands had trembled, whose steps
had been hesitant, as he led her along the corridor.
She'd changed yet again when she'd realized Kate
was in the room, becoming cheerful and teasing. Putting on a show for her cousin.

He mentally cursed. Life, in case anyone hadn't
noticed, could be hell.

Shannon sensed Rory's concern and recoiled. She
wouldn't accept pity from anyone. Holding on to the
smile she'd assumed for Kate, she thanked him again
for the plant and for stopping by.

After he'd left, she exhaled a relieved breath. Being
sociable, especially with Rory, wasn't her thing at the
moment. Besides, she must look like a leftover from
a Saturday-night brawl.

The irony of being concerned about her looks
struck her as she climbed into bed. As if she had
nothing else to worry about except combing her hair
and putting on lipstick.

After handing Kate the robe and letting the fleecy
slippers fall to the floor, she stretched out on the fresh
sheets. She was as tired as a pilgrim returning home
from a long dangerous trip to Mecca.

"Wow," Kate said softly, "Rory Daniels. The
prize catch of the county. Lucky you."

Shannon managed a cheeky grin. "Yeah, should
make local news, don't you think?"

"It's already gone the rounds. I heard he was here
from Betty down at the bank. He'd bought a pot of
poinsettias from the flower shop. Betty's sister, who

works there, told her. I suspect she's told the rest of the town by now.''

Shannon laughed at the absurdity of the notion. Rory had never noticed she existed. Not until he walked into a convenience store and found three bodies on the floor, hers among them, she reflected, the internal darkness drawing around her once more.

The nurse bustled in. ''Mail call,'' she said and laid a new stack of cards in Shannon's lap. ''Well, now, it's nice to hear you laugh. I'll put that on your chart. The doctor will be pleased. This morning he said you could go home if you continued to improve as you have.''

Fear tightened Shannon's throat. ''I can go home?'' she said, immediately worrying about where she would go.

''To the big house,'' Kate said as if reading her mind. ''Megan and Grandfather are expecting you. You can stay with them until the bandages come off and you decide what you want to do next.''

A beat of silence followed this announcement.

''Until we know if I'm blind or not,'' Shannon said, saying what they all were thinking, making herself face the possibility. She felt again the hot flash of pain, the absurdity of being shot by some two-bit crook in a convenience store in a scene straight out of a B movie.

''Now, now, none of that,'' the nurse chided. ''There's every chance you'll be fine. You have to have faith.''

Shannon heard the little squeaks from the woman's

shoes as she arranged a lunch tray on the rolling table. After the woman left, Kate muttered in annoyance, "And a Happy New Year to you, too."

Shannon agreed. "I know she means well, but she is the most irritating person. But I like the mice in her pockets."

"Oh? I didn't notice them," Kate remarked, amusement in her tone.

Shannon explained. She was grateful for Kate's wry humor and the fact that her cousin let her handle her lunch without help. Not that sipping a milk shake through a straw took a lot of skill. Neither did eating the paste that was supposed to be pudding.

Kate read the messages on the get-well cards out loud.

"Can you tell me who the flowers are from?" Shannon asked. "Rory said I had a roomful."

When Kate read Brad's name on a card attached to a vase of pink roses, Shannon perked up.

So he was busy on a case. Or maybe he'd gone to visit his folks in St. Louis this week, although he'd indicated he wasn't going home for the holidays this year.

Reality reared its head. Some people were repulsed by those with a disability. Or scars. That was one worry she hadn't voiced. It seemed so vain compared to everything else, but she had no idea how the wounds would look when they healed.

She would face that when the time came, she promised. Later. When she was alone and could think...

"There, done," Kate said, finishing the cards.

"Thanks." Shannon hesitated, then spoke. "When the doctor came in this morning, he said I'd have to wear the bandages two weeks to give my eyes a good rest. Then..."

"Then we'll know," Kate said quietly.

"Yes."

"Megan and I'll be there for you. You know that."

Shannon nodded, not quite able to envision the future. Fear returned.

Kate kept her entertained with tales of her newly adopted daughter Amanda, Mandy to the family, and Jeremy, Kate's stepson, for the next two hours. When Kate mentioned Jess, her husband of three months, her tone changed, going softer, huskier.

As she listened to Kate's quiet chatter, Shannon thought of Rory Daniels. Maybe he had been the man of cool light who had made her feel safe when she'd been so strangely lost in a hot, dark fog. Or was her dream man only an illusion created out of pain and delirium? Sometimes she still needed him....

"By the way, did Rory tell you he'd bought the place next door to us?" Kate asked when she stood to leave.

"No. What place?"

"The Mulholland land."

The land had belonged to Kate's mother-in-law. Kate's first husband had grown up there. Kris had been several years older than she, a Vietnam vet suffering from post-traumatic stress disorder. One minute he would be fine; the next, he would change into an angry, suspicious man lost in the jungles of his mind, sure the enemy was near and searching for him and his family. It had been eerie. The marriage had ended in Kris's suicide. Kate deserved all the happiness she now had.

"Will Rory live in the house?" Shannon asked, curious since she'd recently had the ancient foreman's cabin on the Windraven Ranch, across the creek from the Mulholland house, remodeled, and had planned to move in over Christmas.

Oh. She was supposed to be out of her apartment in town by the first of the year. "My apartment," she began.

"Megan and I finished moving the last of your things and cleaned it. It's all been taken care of. Your SUV is stored in the garage at the new place, too. Sorry. I should have told you earlier so you wouldn't worry."

"I'd forgotten until this moment." Shannon lifted a hand to her temple.

Kate touched her shoulder, then gave her a kiss on the cheek. "Your mind is fine. Quit worrying."

"It isn't my mind I'm worried about, not really."

"Oh, honey." Kate hugged her fiercely, her protective, nurturing nature familiar and comforting. "We can only wait and see how things turn out. It's hard, I know. You've been terribly brave."

"Hardly. I wanted to ask, has anyone else come to visit that you know of?"

"Like a certain young attorney who's new in town?" Kate teased. Her voice became serious. "Not that I know, but Jess said the sheriff had ordered no visitors other than immediate family. He had a deputy outside your door twenty-four hours a day during the week you were in a coma. He's been pretty worried about you.''

''I guess he thought the robber would sneak in and smother me or something,'' she scoffed, trying not to recall that Rory had somehow gotten in to see her.

Couldn't Brad have found a way?

Maybe. *If he'd loved her.*

There were a lot of ifs in her life just now. She would have to take each day as it came. But she would be okay. She was sure of it.

Chapter Three

Shannon repeated that assurance to everyone who called the rest of the day and the next when Gene Thompson, the sheriff and her boss, came to visit. They discussed the case.

"There was no third man," Shannon told the lawman. "The wounded guy was the perp." She sensed his impatience at her stubborn denial in the silence that followed.

"According to his story, the third man was a customer who came in after you and the store owner were unconscious," Gene said, his gruff voice gentle.

At six feet, six inches and two hundred-plus pounds, the law officer reminded her of a big, friendly bear. Under the tough exterior, he was all heart. He took it hard when one of his deputies was injured.

"They struggled, then the robber shot him and made his getaway?" she asked skeptically.

"Yes."

Shannon mulled over the information. "Well," she finally concluded, "I suppose the evidence shoots holes in my theory that the guy you let go was the robber, especially since the perp's gun wasn't on the premises. I know I shot the real crook. In the shoulder, too, just like the other guy had. The gun couldn't have walked off by itself, and since Rory found three people on the floor, all of us unconscious, the robber must have escaped."

"Yep. With nothing to go on, the case goes onto the back burner."

She hit the flat of her hand on the chair arm. "I wish I could see the store, go over it..." She stopped, then shrugged impatiently, refusing to give way to despair.

"Don't, honey," Gene said softly. "You're going to be fine. Everything has a way of working out."

"Does it?"

"I have to believe that, or else I'd go crazy with the insane things people do. Like shoot people over money." He stood. "Well, it's back to work for me. I understand you'll be going home today."

"Yes, Megan is coming for me as soon as she finishes with her riding students this afternoon. Uh, the nurse said you wouldn't allow any visitors in my room, except family," Shannon said. "And Rory Daniels?"

Gene muttered a curse. "I told them no one other

than Kate and Megan." He snorted, then chuckled. "It's his looks. Women melt when he glances at them. Must be nice."

"I don't know," Shannon said on a lighter note. "It could be hell, having everyone fall all over you."

"Could be. Wind River may not be heaven," the sheriff said, abruptly changing the subject, "but it's still a good place to live. Don't let one incident spoil your life. "

"I won't," Shannon promised, thinking of the cards, flowers and candy she'd received. It had all been disposed of and her room was bare, ready for the next occupant when she left. She wanted to go. Ten days in a hospital was enough for a lifetime.

She kept smiling until the last of her visitors left at the close of visiting hours that afternoon, then she pondered the future. A week from Friday and the bandages would come off. Nine days until she knew her fate. A shaky, rather forlorn, sigh escaped her.

Shannon was surprised when the doctor and the second shift nurse came in a couple of hours later. "What's happening?" she asked, alarmed by the sudden visit.

"We're taking the bandages off," replied the doctor.

Her heart lurched. "Now? I thought it was later."

"Just the ones on your wounds, not the eyes. I don't want any stress on them for a few more days."

"Oh."

When the wrappings came off, her head felt funny.

She reached up to examine the injuries. Feeling a bristly stubble on the left temple, she remarked in surprise, "I'm bald on one side."

The doctor chuckled.

"Not really," the nurse assured her. She was a quiet, efficient person who spoke in a normal, friendly manner. "If you had bangs around your face and a layered look on the sides, the short hair would blend in with the rest in a couple of weeks."

"Thanks. I'll do that."

After they left, Shannon found her brush and fussed with her hair. She wondered when she could shower. She must look terrible. On an impulse, she called the beauty shop.

Marilee said she would give her a shampoo and a cut whenever she appeared. "Don't worry about other customers," she said airily. "They can wait."

Shannon felt better after hanging up the phone. She'd punched in the number without help. Her spirits lifted. It was a beginning. Today the telephone. Tomorrow the world!

She laughed until she realized she was close to tears. That wouldn't do, not at all. She wasn't going to get all weepy and make people worry about her when the doctor didn't know anything yet. Besides, everything was going to be fine.

When Megan arrived, Shannon was ready to go, and they took off for home.

"Umm, the air smells so crisp and fresh," Shannon said.

She found she could tell where they were by using

her other senses. She recognized the clatter of the tires on the old trestle bridge when they went over the creek. She heard the cows at a dairy farm. The scent of incense cedar indicated the woods near the house.

When they arrived, she eagerly got out of the station wagon and waited for her cousin. She'd experienced a sense of vulnerability at leaving the known haven of the hospital, but now she wanted freedom from restrictions and routine.

"It snowed last night. The sun is out today and everything looks pristine," Megan had told her. "Hold on. I'm coming as soon as I get myself together. It's really cold today. It'll be well below freezing tonight."

Shannon waited for Megan to take her arm and lead her into the house. Lifting her face to the sun, she pictured the mountains, elegant in their coats of new snow. She loved the hills and the sense of family that came to her each time she returned to the ranch. Her roots were buried deep within the rocky soil.

With a painful lurch of her heart, she realized she might never see the place again. The hot darkness descended on her, as if someone had thrown a blanket over her head. She breathed carefully and fought for composure.

"Can you carry your personal belongings? Your gun's inside the bag. Careful. The flagstones may be slippery." Megan put a plastic bag into her hand and took her arm.

Shannon pulled herself back from the brink of panic. She walked through the snow to the side door of the sprawling two-story ranch house, guided by Megan's touch and voice. "Here're the steps. Up. Up. Let me get the door open. Okay, let's go inside."

"Home," Shannon murmured when the door closed behind her. "It's good to be here." She inhaled the scent of fresh pine and cinnamon in the air. "Something smells good."

"I made spiced cider before I left to pick you up. Kate sent over apple fritters. Mrs. Roddey cut some pine boughs and put them on the hearth."

Mrs. Roddey was wife to the rancher who leased their land. "Where's Grandfather?" Shannon stuck her gloves in her pocket, then hung her coat on the hall tree without help.

"He lay down for a nap a little bit ago. I think the worry over you has gotten to him. He's looked sort of peaked the past few days."

"Maybe Christmas was hard on him. It is for many people. It makes them feel lonely."

"Go into the parlor," Megan suggested. "I'll take care of these bags and things."

Shannon touched the door with her right hand, then, going on memory, walked into the parlor, which was the family gathering place.

The warmth of a fire in the fireplace reached out to her as she carefully felt for the glider rocker and took a seat. She exhaled a ragged sigh, as if she'd finally reached a safe place after an arduous trip. She hated the feeling of uncertainty, of being vulnerable—

"You did that very well," a masculine voice commented.

Shannon gripped the arms of the chair. "Brad?"

"Sorry to disappoint you," the man said with sardonic amusement. "Rory Daniels. I came by to check on a couple of Megan's boarders and stayed to welcome you home."

Shannon realized how ungracious she'd sounded. "Oh, yes, the Good Samaritan. Thank you again for your help."

She realized Rory must be in the chair that used to be her grandfather's. Sitting in the big leather recliner, her granddad used to read the Christmas story from the Bible every year on Christmas Eve. That was before the stroke that had left him paralyzed.

Things, times, people changed. A wise person accepted that fact. But it was hard.

"Don't mention it. As a doctor, I'm dedicated to healing, no matter what kind of animal crosses my path."

Was it her imagination or was his tone decidedly cooler than his earlier greeting? Had she offended him by thanking him for his help?

"That's very commendable," she replied with the exact inflection he'd used on her, irritated without knowing why.

There was a brief silence. "Your hair looks nice," he commented.

Shannon's hand flew to the bristly section at her temple. "I had it shampooed and cut before I let Megan bring me home. Marilee said it would blend okay in a few days."

"It looks great now. You can hardly tell one side is shorter than the other."

She didn't want to ask, but there was something she'd worried over during the hours when she couldn't sleep for thinking about the future. She thought he would tell her the truth. "What about the wound? Can you see where the bullet went in or...or anything?"

She hated the hesitation, as if she was afraid of his answer. She squared her shoulders and waited.

When he moved from the chair, she felt a stir of air near her face. Warmth touched her an instant before he did.

Fingers caressed the side of her jaw before sliding under her chin and lifting her face. She stared up at him, or where she imagined him to be.

She was wrong. When he spoke, she realized his face was nearly level with hers and very close. His breath caressed her cheek as he answered.

"The scar at your temple won't be visible. Your hair will cover it completely when it grows another half inch. Now under your chin..."

She waited, her breath shallow, for his pronouncement.

"That might be noticed if someone is specifically looking for it, or if they happen to be at this level with your head tilted just so. Otherwise, it isn't obvious. The surgeon did an excellent job of stitching it up."

Her breath rushed out in audible relief. Feeling self-conscious, she tried to laugh. That sounded even worse.

"Nothing like being vain," she finally managed.

"Everyone is," he said softly, "to a certain extent. No one wants to feel like a freak."

His tone was deep, with an unexpected huskiness that surprised and disturbed her. He'd sounded amused, cynical, maybe bitter, but also gentle and understanding. Which didn't fit her image of him at all.

"Well, that's one worry you've certainly never had," she said, injecting wry amusement in her voice.

"Haven't I?"

Wondering what he meant, she instinctively reached toward him, as if to check for herself that he was as she remembered. She encountered his lean cheek and chiseled jawline. He had classical good looks, the bone structure strong and masculine, his nose straight, his lips…she tried to think of a descriptive word and failed.

She traced the outline of his mouth with her fingertips. His lips were warm, firm and yet surprisingly soft. When they moved slightly under her touch, a tingle of electricity zinged up her arm.

She drew back, startled.

Her unthinking action was too intimate. She'd invaded his personal space. "I'm sorry. I don't know what came over me, to touch you like that."

A hand caught her wrist and brought her hand into contact with the warm flesh again. "Go ahead," he invited. "I like being touched. By you," he added in a very soft voice, as if it were a surprising after-thought.

Thus encouraged, she outlined his nose, ran a finger over each eyebrow, then glided over his forehead to his hair. The strands felt crisp and clean under her hand.

She knew it was inky black. So were his eyebrows and lashes. His eyes were a light, pure blue. It was a startling combination and extremely attractive.

The scent of shampoo and aftershave came to her. His cheek was smooth to her touch as if he'd show-ered and shaved recently. She thought how it might be if they kissed—

"You're as handsome as ever," she reported, drop-ping her hands to her lap, feeling foolish and inept in a way she hadn't felt since her first date.

He stood and moved away.

Toward the fireplace, she surmised. His tall—six-two or so—frame blocked its warmth. Odd, but she sensed something was bothering him. She couldn't imagine what.

Rory was a man who had it all—looks, money, respect, the career he'd chosen even though she'd heard his father had wanted him to go into law. What was his problem?

It occurred to her that he'd never married. He'd dated various women, none of them for long, accord-ing to local gossip. Why settle for one when so many were available?

The black depression returned. Hearing Megan's footsteps, she was glad he'd moved away. An odd picture they would have made, her exploring his face as if she'd never seen the man before.

And him letting her...even encouraging it.

Well, weirder things had probably happened. She clasped her hands tightly in her lap and felt the tingle lightly play over her fingertips and up her arm again. She'd never felt that before, not just from touching someone.

"Why don't you stay for dinner?" Megan said to Rory, coming into the room. "Grandfather would love to have a man to talk to for a change. He and I rattle around the house like two lost souls most nights. That's why I'm delighted Shannon's here. She can entertain us now with wild exciting tales of her work."

"Thanks, I'd like that. I imagine Shannon's had some interesting experiences," Rory said.

"Well, nothing else as exciting as the robbery and 'shoot-out,'" she said, using the media's term with a large dollop of droll humor.

Megan and Rory laughed at her stories as she recounted some of the odd things people did in unexpected situations—like the man who carried the cash register out of his burning store and set it on the hood of his burning car.

To her surprise, the next hour passed quickly. She even began to relax as Rory took up the conversational reins and amused them with stories of pets and their owners.

She found herself listening intently. There were nuances in people's voices she hadn't noticed before...

such as the husky, sexy quality in the masculine baritone. A tingle raced along her scalp and down her neck.

A noise came from down the hall. "Here's Grandfather," Megan announced, rising. "Rory is staying for dinner with us," she told the older man. "I told him you would be glad of some male company."

Shannon felt her grandfather's kiss on her cheek, then heard him greet Rory in a guttural tone, the words indistinct.

Rory chatted easily, relating news of the ranches around the valley and the people on them, all known to the Windoms for years and years. He'd always been a polite person when they met, even when they argued over local issues, but now she saw—realized, she corrected—that he was a considerate one, too.

He told of his plans to breed an Olympic champion. "Big pie-in-the-sky plans," he admitted with a self-deprecating chuckle. "But if you're going to dream, it might as well be a big dream as a small one."

"I agree," Megan put in.

"What's your dream?" Shannon asked. She and her cousin, only a year younger and her best friend, had shared everything as teenagers. As adults, they had put aside long, heart-searching discussions for the realities of living.

Megan laughed. "I want to ride that Olympic champion for Rory."

Shannon pictured the other two working together on their common goal. They would probably fall in love and marry. Their children would be beautiful....

Loneliness swept over her with no warning, a terrible desolate sense of isolation. No one would want her—

With an effort, she pulled herself back from the brink of morbid self-pity. That wouldn't do, not at all.

For the rest of the evening, the conversation flowed among the three of them. Her grandfather surprised her by managing to make a few comments, an improvement over his usual silent presence.

He'd been through ten years of living in a wheelchair, barely able to communicate during that time, all without a whimper. She'd never seen *him* cry over his fate. Clenching her hand into a fist, she vowed to be as brave, no matter what happened nine days from now.

A hand touched her clenched one, lightly, briefly.

She realized it was Rory's, seated at her left. Turning towards him, she smiled to show him she was fine.

''Atta girl,'' he murmured next to her ear, startling her at how close he was.

After dinner, their guest insisted on helping Megan clean up. While they had someone come in occasionally to clean the house and watch after Grandfather, they couldn't afford full-time help.

A five-thousand acre ranch was expensive to run but brought in little money. Thanks to Kate, the place was solvent, but for a while after her Uncle Sean's death, the cousins had thought they might lose it.

Shannon worried that she would now be an added expense on the household budget. She needed to find a way to make a living. Others managed, she reminded herself, as she mentally cringed at the idea of facing people without being able to see their gestures and expressions.

Besides, she'd be able to see with her right eye at the very least. She was sure of it.

But just in case, what could she do?

While the conversation ebbed and flowed around her, she contemplated the future. As a psychologist, she didn't have to have sight. She could record her sessions and dictate her notes. It would be more difficult but not impossible.

"Don't you think so, Shannon?" Megan asked.

"What? I'm sorry. I wasn't listening."

From her left came the sound of a deep chuckle. Rory said, "We were discussing a partnership, Megan and I. We think it makes sense to combine our efforts on a horse-breeding program."

"To produce an Olympic champ?" she asked.

"Right," he said, not at all embarrassed about revealing his dreams of the future.

Shannon put aside her own worries and considered. Rory might be good for Megan. Her cousin spent way too much of her time alone or with the kids in the riding classes she taught or with their grandfather.

"It makes sense. I mean, you're both experts with horses. Besides, it would save you an enormous amount of money in vet bills," she told her cousin, then realized how crass that sounded.

He laughed as if delighted with this practical observation. "Well, then, that settles it. We have official endorsement from the sheriff's department."

A wisp of memory floated into her mind. A voice. Deep. Soothing. Reassuring. Someone—a man, she knew that—had examined her with hands so gentle she'd longed to see his face. His touch had been cool on her hot forehead and at her temple. When she'd opened her eyes and tried to see him, she'd been blinded by the brilliant light that had surrounded him like a halo.

"The weather is supposed to be nice tomorrow," Rory continued. "Let's go riding. The mare that had the inflamed leg needs some light exercise, and I want to see how she handles herself with other horses."

Silence ensued after the invitation.

Shannon assumed Megan was thinking it over. A hand nudged her arm.

"Hey, you gone to sleep?" he asked.

"Are you talking to me?"

"Yeah. I know Megan wants to go. How about you?"

Fear rushed over her. "I—I don't know. I hadn't thought about it."

"You need to get out," he said decisively. "Don't worry. We'll watch out so you don't fall down a gopher hole."

Shannon heard Megan gasp. "Rory," she scolded.

"I wanted her to know it won't be a case of the blind leading the blind," he said blandly. "Unless she's scared, or doesn't trust us to watch after her."

Shannon's hackles rose. "I've been riding horses

since I could sit up by myself. I'd hardly be afraid of one. Especially if Megan is with me.''

There, that would let him know her faith was in her cousin, not a handsome charmer like him.

''Good. I'll be over around noon or whenever I finish at the clinic.'' He paused. ''It *is* okay for her to ride, isn't it?''

''Well, the doctor didn't say she was under any restrictions on activities,'' Megan told him. ''At least, not to me.''

''Nor to me,'' Shannon informed them briskly, determined to speak for herself. After all, she wasn't an invalid.

The clock on the mantel chimed ten times. Shannon hadn't realized it was so late. Fatigue rolled over her. It had been a very long day. Her emotions had gyrated through several ups and downs.

''Grandfather is ready to go to his room,'' Megan announced. ''I'll make us some cocoa and be back shortly.''

Shannon kissed her grandfather's cheek when he stopped by the rocker and patted her knee. ''Good night,'' she murmured to the patriarch, again experiencing a fierce protective love for her family.

''What makes you sad?'' Rory asked when the other two were gone.

''I was thinking of my grandfather. He's outlived his wife and all three of his children. That must be a terribly lonely thing for a person. Then to have a stroke and be confined in a wheelchair seems so unfair.''

"Yeah, it's tough. But so is he. And you."

She smoothed the hair over her temple and managed a smile. "I'm not so sure—"

"I am."

"Listen, about tomorrow." She paused, trying to figure out how to say what she was thinking. "You don't have to…to keep an eye on me. I mean, you're under no obligation to watch after me—"

"I never thought I was."

"What I'm trying to say is that…well, I know you found me and saved my life and all, but you don't have to feel responsible for me. You don't have to check on me. After all, I'm not your patient," she ended stoically.

He snorted, made a strangling sound, then burst into unabashed laughter.

She realized how stupid she'd sounded. "Okay, so I made a donkey of myself. You know what I meant."

He stifled the chortles. "Yes, I know. I don't feel I have to look after you."

She heard him move, then felt his touch on her cheek. She held very still while her heart set up a heavy, alarmed pounding. Fear, unlike that experienced during the past ten days, fluttered through her chest.

"But you do have the most kissable mouth of any woman I've ever met," he murmured in an oddly quiet tone, almost as if he spoke to himself.

Her breath hung in her throat, then she laughed. "You suddenly noticed this? That's a bit hard to swallow when we've lived in the same town all our lives.''

''Yeah,'' he agreed. ''Sometimes it takes an incident to change fate, so to speak. Like seeing a person on a snowy night with Christmas lights sparkling in her eyes.''

He touched her temple next to the patch over her left eye. When she felt warmth near her mouth, she gasped, unable to believe what she thought was about to happen.

Then his mouth was there, increasing the warmth to heat, then fire.

Stunned, she couldn't move, couldn't think. Except for one question. Why had she ever thought of him as a person of coolness? His touch was that of the sun, radiating warmth clear down to her toes.

Confusion swept over her.

Now he was one with the dark, swirling fog that had haunted her the week of the coma, with the longing that had invaded her soul as she'd searched for a way out of the hot darkness, with the awful need for another person that frightened her because it felt too dangerous.

''Don't,'' she whispered.

He drew back slightly. ''I can't help it. Your lips are too tempting.''

His mouth touched hers again. His hands stroked through her hair. She hesitated, then, unable to stop, leaned into the kiss, letting it take her, needing the healing touch—

''No,'' she said and jerked away.

He didn't insist, but she could sense his gaze on her. "That was an experiment," he said finally.

"To prove what?"

"To see if it was need or desire."

The admission caught her off guard. "Which was it?"

His brief laugh was rueful. "Both."

When he moved away, she was relieved. And disappointed. "Here's Megan," she said, hearing her cousin's footsteps in the hall.

"Saved," he murmured wickedly.

The aroma of hot cocoa preceded the other woman into the room. "It's really cold out tonight," she said. "You might want to warm your truck before heading home."

"I'll be fine," Rory said. "It isn't far and the cocoa will keep me warm enough on the way."

Shannon's face felt hot. There had been nuances in his simple statement, in the huskiness of his voice, that told her he was thinking of more than hot chocolate.

When he finished and left, Shannon stood, too. "I think I'll go to bed. My usual room?" she asked.

"Yes. Do you need any help? Kate lectured me about letting you do for yourself, so I'm trying to be good."

Shannon laughed. "You're doing great. I can get myself to bed."

Later, after she'd washed up and slipped into her flannel pajamas, she sat on the bed, too tense to think of sleep. Sensing warmth, she discovered the light was on. The bed had been turned back, too. Megan's doing.

After flicking off the unnecessary light, she lingered with her hand on the bedside phone. Finally she lifted the receiver and slowly, carefully punched in a number.

It rang once.

She started to hang up, but then it was answered.

"Hello?" Brad said, obviously irritated at the call.

"Who is it?" someone said in the background.

A woman.

Shannon hung up very quietly and sat there in the utter stillness of the winter night. She wanted to believe there was some mistake, that she'd dialed the wrong number, but she knew she hadn't.

He could have called. He could have asked how she was, then casually mentioned that he'd met an old friend while working on a case, anything to let her know there was someone else.

The loneliness enclosed her, and she sat there for a long time in the darkness, her mind carefully blank, her heart beating steadily as if she had all eternity to contemplate, rather than this moment that felt like betrayal.

But, she reminded herself in all honesty, there had been no understanding between them, no commitment...no love.

Lying down and pulling the covers up to her chin, she tried to see through the blackness and find a future that seemed possible. It was scary to be so alone.

Her cousins thought she was brave, but she wasn't.

Only Rory seemed to sense the moments when despair came too close and it became an effort to smile.

The memory of a cool, gentle touch at her temple, the tingling sensation of warm lips against her fingertips, the surprise in a stolen kiss, came to her.

The darkness seemed to lessen, and she felt comforted. It was the oddest thing....

Chapter Four

Rory spotted Shannon straddling the rail fence of a paddock when he arrived shortly after noon the next day. Megan was working with a young stud she was training for a rich dude who, in his opinion, had no business trying to raise horses. The man was rarely at his vanity ranch, as the locals called it, and was totally inept when it came to ranching and livestock.

After parking next to the stable, Rory clipped a fanny pack around his hips. It contained the lunch he'd missed by coming out here. He joined Shannon at the fence.

"Good morning. Rory, isn't it?" she said.

Her smile was bright enough, yet he sensed the uncertainty that she carefully hid. There was the slightest hint of a tremor in her hands as she toyed with the zipper on her jacket. It made his chest give that painful twang that was becoming disturbingly familiar whenever he was around her…or thought of her…or remembered how soft her mouth was…or… Enough of those thoughts. They made him hot and hard.

"Yeah. What gave me away?"

"First your truck. I thought I recognized the engine. Then your footsteps. You have a longer stride than anyone else I recognize. I also know Megan's in the paddock, so that leaves you as the prime suspect."

He smiled, then realizing she couldn't see it, chuckled at her reasoning. "Spoken like a true cop. You ready for a ride down to the lake?"

She cocked her head saucily. "I'm not sure. How will I know which end of the horse is the front?"

He sucked in a harsh breath. She looked particularly beautiful with the sun picking out the red-gold tints in her hair, which flowed past her shoulders in graceful waves. He wanted to touch it.

"Grab one end and give a yank," he suggested. "He'll let you know which end you got a hold of."

She burst into surprised laughter at his advice. "I don't think I want to get into a debate with an indignant horse. He can kick harder than I can."

"I won't let you get into trouble," he promised. "Hey, Meg, you ready to go?"

Megan declined. "Tinseltown Johnny is acting up. I don't think I'll trust him on the trail. You and Shannon go on. I've saddled your mounts. They're on the other side of the stable."

"You're going to miss a great lunch. I had the diner pack us some barbecue sandwiches."

She wrinkled her nose at him, then had to concentrate to stay in the saddle as the young stallion plunged and snorted. Six months of expert training would be undone in six weeks of riding by the cowboy dude. Too bad. The stud had good conformation and excellent bloodlines.

"You ready?" he asked Shannon.

"Maybe we should go some other time," she suggested.

He realized she really was nervous. In fact, she seemed very ill at ease this morning, much more than last night. He paused and wondered if it had been that rash kiss.

"Don't worry," he said with forced casualness. "I won't pounce on you without warning."

Looking at her perched on the fence, he admitted he still had a mad desire to grab her and kiss that pert mouth into sweet, wild response....

Whoa. Let's not go there, he cautioned his libido. Consider this a good deed for the day, not a lover's tryst.

"Come on, no arguments."

Reaching up, he slipped his hands under her down jacket and clasped her waist. He was surprised at how tiny she was. Again, as in the hospital, he sensed her vulnerability. It puzzled him. He pulled her forward, valiantly resisting a strong urge to crush her against his chest.

"Oh," she said and instinctively threw her hands out to catch herself.

She whacked him right in the nose. "Ouch." He set her on her feet and examined the injured part.

"I'm sorry. What happened?" she asked anxiously. "Did I hurt you? I didn't mean to."

He started laughing. "It wasn't your fault. I should have told you what I was doing instead of thinking about how much I wanted to ravish you."

A hand flew to her mouth. She stared up at him as if she had X-ray vision and could see through the black eye patches. Finally, "You're weird," she told him sternly.

"Well, if you knew how sexy those eye patches are, you wouldn't think that. Kissing a lady pirate should be almost as exciting as kissing a lady cop."

"Yeah, well, you'd better behave, or I'll handcuff you to a post and leave you."

He took her arm and led her away. "I'll try. My word is my pledge, ma'am, so I'm not making any out-and-out promises on my future behavior."

After a pause, she laughed, as if deciding to take the hunger he couldn't quite ignore as a joke. In the pasture on the other side of the stable, he found a piebald gelding and the mare, saddled and ready to go.

"I'm going to lift you up, so don't go flailing around with those dangerous fists, okay?"

"I'll try to restrain myself."

Her laughter sounded more natural this time. Maybe she had decided to trust him.

When they were on their way—her on the mare with the convalescing leg—he noticed her head tilted to one side as if listening intently while she tried to figure out a puzzle.

"We're riding south toward the lake," he told her. "I thought we'd stay in the sun and soak up some warmth. The temperature is around thirty-five."

"But no wind to add a chill factor," she said. "That's good. It feels wonderful to be out and about again."

The smile disappeared and she became pensive as they rode farther across the sixty-acre pasture that led to the path to the lake. He left her to her thoughts. His own were troublesome enough.

Maybe she'd thought he was joking about the ravishing part, but he wasn't. His libido was acting up in a most curious fashion. Since his earlier experiences with other women, he'd maintained strict discipline in that department. Adults should be able to control their baser instincts, especially when it came to forcing them on people who weren't interested.

He studied his riding companion. "You have good hands and a natural seat," he complimented her.

"I feel rather stiff. I'm afraid he's going to make a move I won't anticipate in time."

"He's a she. Haven't you ever been thrown?"

"Oh, yes. The memory of the last time is what's making me so cautious. Megan asked me to practice a steeplechase with her so her horse would get used to being crowded at the jumps. My horse stopped at one. I didn't.''

Her dimples winked at him when she compressed the corners of her mouth to subdue a wry grin when he laughed. A burst of warmth spread through him like a shot of brandy on an empty stomach. Glancing down, he was glad she couldn't see the ridge behind his fly as his body hardened with hunger, or else she might have had second or third thoughts about riding out alone with him.

Actually, since moving to a larger office and buying the small ranch near here, he hadn't had time to even think of the opposite sex, so his reaction surprised him.

"We're coming up to the gate," he warned when they neared the end of the pasture. "I'll open it and let you through, then close it. We'll have a picnic by the lake."

"Is it frozen over?"

"Not yet. There's ice out to six or eight feet from the shore, but not in the middle yet. There will be soon if it stays as cold as it has been recently."

"We used to ice-skate here. Kate and Aunt Bunny taught me and Megan. It was such fun."

"Bunny. She was Megan's mother, wasn't she?"

"Yes."

He was sorry he'd said anything. Shannon looked sad as he opened and closed the gate for them. Her aunt had drowned in a boating accident. In silence, they rode down to the water's edge. A gazebo with a picnic table free of snow beckoned. That was their destination.

"Here we are." He swung down from the saddle and tied the gelding to one of the sturdy gazebo rails.

Shannon dismounted before he could help her. She felt around in front of her, found the rail and tied up, too.

"You did that very well," he told her.

"I remember this place. We came here often as kids. It was a playhouse, fort, ship, stage. Megan and I used to put on terrific shows. We danced and sang to our own made-up songs. Kate was our audience."

"I'd have liked to have seen that. Maybe you'll sing for me after lunch."

"No way. I sound worse than a frog with a bug in its throat. Megan has the voice in our family. She probably could have made it as an entertainer."

"I didn't know that." He escorted her to the picnic table with a hand at the small of her back. "Three steps," he warned when they came to them. "I'll make a snow well for our drinks."

He gathered two piles of snow from a railing and made holders for the two cans of soda, then put out the sandwiches and chips.

"Umm, kosher dill pickles from the café one of my favorite things," she said.

He paused. "How did you know that?"

"I can smell them." She opened the wrapping on the sandwich. "You know, it's true that your other senses seem to become stronger when one is shut off. I think it's because you concentrate on them. I find myself really listening to what's going on around me since the robbery. I notice scents more, too.''

''So do I,'' he murmured, thinking of her.

''I know a lot of people by their movements and footsteps now whereas I never noticed before. I wonder if I will after they take the patches off.''

When I can see again, was the unspoken assumption behind that statement.

''What will you do if you can't see?'' he asked quietly.

Her lips trembled before she pressed them together. He suppressed an urge to take her into his arms. He'd want to do more than merely comfort her.

''Well,'' she began, a shade of uncertainty in the word, ''I hope to start my practice—''

''Practice?''

''Family counseling. I need to write my dissertation, then I'll have a Ph.D. in psychology. I already have all my notes in order.''

When her voice faltered, Rory gave her a quick glance.

''Assuming anyone will want to consult with me,'' she finished with a wry grimace.

''You'll need someone to read your notes,'' he said. ''You can probably hire a teenager for a reasonable sum to come over in the afternoons. Kids love to earn extra money, especially at easy jobs.''

''Yes.'' Her smile bloomed once more. ''That's a good idea. If I need help,'' she added. ''There's a fifty-fifty chance that...that it'll be okay.''

''Yeah, that's what Kate said.''

They ate in silence for a few minutes. He noticed she wiped her mouth often. It occurred to him that a barbecue sandwich might not have been the best choice in her situation, but she was handling it fine.

Admiration grew in him. It wasn't a familiar emotion in regard to women. He'd respected his mother. And Kate. Megan since he'd come to know her. A few others who had treated him as a person rather than a prize. Now this woman.

Even if she ended up blind, he knew she would make it. The three cousins had determination and grit. Shannon had something more. An inner fire that caused a very definite spark in him. She didn't seem to know it.

He pictured her as she'd looked that evening on the street, leading the little parade of children across, a sparkle in her eyes, as if all of life existed in her.

Her eyes...they were blue, he suddenly recalled. With a touch of gray. Smoky. Sexy.

He took a breath, finished off the soda and packed their debris away. He needed movement, exercise, anything to divert the direction of his thinking. "How about a walk by the lake?"

"Okay." She rose and waited.

He took her hand, tucked it in the crook of his elbow and started off. However, he forgot to warn her about the steps this time.

When she tumbled forward, he leaped in front of her, pivoted on one foot and grabbed her before she could fall. Holding her in his arms, he stepped down the final step to the safety of the ground.

She clutched the lapels of his old bomber jacket, her breath coming fast between parted lips. Fear was replaced by confusion on her expressive face. He'd never realized that a mouth could tell a watchful person so much about another.

"I'm—I'm sorry," she said in a near whisper.

"It was my fault."

He didn't let her go, but stood there, the sun warm on his back, her in his arms. She was on the step above him, her mouth at a level with his and no more than six inches away. He only had to lean his head forward a little.

Don't, he warned, but he knew he wasn't going to heed the warning.

Dipping his head, he touched her lips. They trembled slightly under his, then she pressed them firmly together. It was a challenge he couldn't ignore. He wanted movement, response, not denial.

He caressed them lightly again. With his tongue, he traced their outline. He liked their soft, lush feel against his lips. "You have the sexiest lips. Soft. Very feminine."

"I…"

When her lips parted, he didn't let her finish the statement. Instead, he took the kiss deeper without thinking about it. He ran his tongue along the edge of her teeth, then dipped inside. Her taste was incredibly sweet.

And exhilarating.

Shannon inhaled deeply, seeking stability when she felt shaky and confused. His aroma engulfed her in balsam, a lime aftershave, horses, leather and the great outdoors, reminding her of the scent of fresh, crisp air and cold brilliant light on snow.

Flashing back in time, she knew when she'd last experienced this. Sometime after the shooting. When she'd been tormented by blinding heat. Someone had touched her with hands so cool, they had soothed the hot ache in her head. When she'd opened her eyes, she'd seen only a brilliant burst of light surrounding him before she'd slipped into the darkness again. And blue. Something blue.

Joy flashed through her. She knew his touch. This was her guardian angel. Sighing, she reached for him, needing, welcoming the pure bliss of his embrace. At last…at last she was safe.

When her arms slipped around his neck and she gave a tiny moan of pleasure, Rory thought of home and bed just a short ride around the edge of the lake, no more than a half mile. Or that the picnic table would do.

Shocked that he'd gone from a simple kiss to thinking of bed and more in a flash, he eased back from the kiss.

Shannon frowned in protest. She didn't want to give this up, not just yet. It was too wonderful, soothing and exciting at the same time. Different from anything she'd ever experienced. Wanting it to last, she clutched the cool leather of his jacket and pressed upward.

With a soft groan, he caught her to him in a sweet hard embrace. His mouth became more urgent on hers. Leaning into him, she felt the hard evidence of his hunger. Pleasurable need shot through her, surprising her. She hadn't thought she was a sensual person.

But she could be, she realized a second before the hazy fog of desire engulfed her completely.

"I want…" She didn't know how to say it.

"I know," he murmured huskily. The need was a deep hot hunger in him, too, passion so strong he marveled at it. "So do I. More than I ever thought possible."

Shannon felt his hands move behind her back, then his bare fingers raked through her hair, cupping the back of her neck. She tugged off one glove, too, and touched the side of his face. His skin was cool to her palm, then it was warm.

"But…why?" she asked, again experiencing the peculiar confusion he caused in her, the strange exciting combination of warmth and coolness.

His lips touched her temple, her ear, a sensitive spot under it. "Madness," he whispered, supplying an answer. "From the moment I saw you on the street."

She held his head between her hands, covering his ears to keep them warm. "You should wear a hat," she scolded with a great deal of tenderness. She didn't understand that feeling, either.

"Hate them, always have."

He opened their jackets. The momentary rush of cold air didn't cool his blood. Then it was gone, replaced by the warmth of her body against his.

In spite of the hunger, he again had an impression of her slenderness, of how vulnerable she was at this moment to any demands he might make. And of how wrong it was for him to make them.

With an effort, he eased back from the kiss. A frown nicked two faint lines over the bridge of her nose. She pushed closer. He pressed his face into her clean shiny hair and held her, simply held her.

He regretted the moment sanity returned and she pulled away from him.

"I'm sorry," she said in a husky voice. "I don't know what...what came over me."

He quieted a bark of sardonic laughter. She was sincere. It was the damnedest thing—a woman apologizing to him for her passion.

"The same thing that came over me, darlin'," he told her lightly. "We have a thing for each other, it seems."

Shannon listened intently to the intonations of his voice. Humor, an edgy, sardonic anger—only a trace, but still there—and the hardness of resolve, as if he'd decided it wouldn't happen again.

For another moment, they stood there, facing each other like combatants in a fierce battle in which they were the only two survivors.

"We'd better go for that walk, then get back," she said. She licked her lips, which felt warm and rosy. A momentary sadness riffled through her. To find this mind-blowing passion now seemed unfair.

He certainly didn't want to get involved with her, and she didn't want to be involved with anyone. Not at the present. She had a future to figure out, once she knew what it was going to be.

Taking a deep breath, she forced herself to face facts. No sane man would want the burden of a blind or even partially blind wife. For a moment, lost in this man's arms, she had overlooked that fact, but now she was thinking straight again.

"Right." Rory lightly touched her on the shoulder. "Uh, I don't usually accost women without warning," he said by way of apology for his unthinking actions.

"But you do after giving sufficient notice?" she asked with mock seriousness, remembering he'd said something similar back at the paddock, then she spoiled it by grinning.

Her smile, her humor, her courage, made Rory want to kiss her all over again. He frowned, angry with himself. She was basically helpless and in his care, although she didn't seem to realize that fact.

What kind of man took advantage of a woman in her situation?

He didn't like the answer.

"You're quiet," Megan said at dinner.

Shannon laid her fork on the plate of beef stew Mrs. Roddey had sent over for their dinner. "I'm rather tired. All that fresh air, I suppose."

"Or the excitement of being with Rory," Megan teased.

"Oh, well, there is that," Shannon returned without disclosing any emotion.

She swallowed hard as a ball of confusion formed in her throat. She'd tried all afternoon to explain that episode between her and Rory down by the lake. Heat, like a tiny pulsating sun, had lingered deep inside her since their passionate kisses, sending uneasy waves of hunger through her each time she thought about them.

Odder still had been *his* desire.

This from the man every single female, and maybe some attached ones, in the county would have sold her soul for. This from the man who could have anyone.

Had he felt sorry for her?

Had she reacted out of gratitude to the man who had rescued her from the burning pain of her wounds and saved her life?

"How did the mare do?" Megan continued after a minute.

"Fine. Rory should be able to give you a more detailed report."

"I wanted to check with him, but he unsaddled your mounts, put them in the pasture and left before I got a chance. He must have been late getting back for his afternoon office hours."

"Probably." Shannon spoke to her grandfather. "Shall we listen to the CD from the *Phantom of the Opera* tonight? If I remember correctly, it's one of your favorites."

"And yours," Megan said. "You two go to the parlor. I'll put on the music, then clean up the dishes."

"I can help with them—"

"Don't be silly. The doctor said you were to take it easy for a few more days."

Eight more days, Shannon thought, her hand going to the bandages on her eyes. A shiver ran over her, reminding her of the fear that seemed to lurk close by, ready to grab at her when she let her guard down.

Taking hold of the back of her grandfather's wheelchair for guidance, Shannon followed him into the other room. Megan had already built a fire. Shannon felt its warmth as soon as she entered.

"Megan is thoughtful," she remarked, settling in the rocker. "So is Kate."

"You, too," Grandfather assured her in the guttural tones so different from the powerful masculine voice she recalled from childhood.

Back then, she'd thought her granddad spoke with the voice of God, or at least very close to how God would have sounded had He ever had occasion to speak directly to her.

She smiled at the childish fantasy. So much had changed since those days when she'd thought life was perfect. Except for the third grade. Her teacher had been a witch until her father had gone and talked to the woman, then she'd been nice the rest of the year. Then had come fourth grade. That was the year her father had left. The bitterness of past disappointments revived. She would be wise to watch her heart when Rory was around.

"Tell me about your childhood," she requested of her grandfather. "Did you ride like the wind? Mother said you were the best man on the ranch at riding and roping, that you could gentle a horse with just a touch.''

"It was a long time ago," he said, his words slow and hesitant, as if he had to think about each one before he said it.

Maybe he didn't want to remember those days when he had been young and carefree, when he could still stride across the land he loved. Her heart went out to him. Life could be so cruel.

Later, when the older man had gone to bed and she and Megan were alone, she said, "I wonder why Grandfather never married again after Grandmother died. He was only in his forties at the time, what, forty-five or six?"

"Forty-six. Maybe it was because he was still in love with Sunny Herriot's wife."

Shannon heard Megan add wood to the fire and use the poker on it. "I never believed that old tale," she said. "Grandmother was a wonderful person. Why would he want anyone else?"

Megan resumed her seat in the leather chair before answering. "I heard someone gossiping about it after my father's funeral. Losing his first love to a Herriot—they were engaged, you know—that's why he's hated them all these years, according to the story.''

"How sad," Shannon said, thinking of the pain her grandfather must have felt. It hurt her to think of it. Since her injury, she seemed to be much more sensitive to other people's feelings.

"So. Tell me about your trip with Rory. You two were gone an awfully long time. Where did you go?"

This much Shannon could talk about without hesitation. "Down by the lake. We ate lunch at the table in the gazebo. Remember it?"

Megan laughed softly. "Yes. We used to put on the most awful shows."

"Well, we thought we were great."

"Kate used to suffer through them and applaud after every song and dance routine."

"She sometimes joined in," Shannon reminded her cousin, laughing at their antics. She sighed. "It was idyllic, wasn't it?"

"Yes—" Megan stopped abruptly. "Shannon," she said in a disbelieving voice. "Shannon, I remember…"

"What?" Shannon asked quietly, hardly daring to move. Megan didn't remember anything of her first eleven years. At the time of her mother's death in a boating accident, she had totally lost all memory of the past up to that point.

Megan let out a shaky breath. "Only that we danced and made up silly songs. I wish it would all come back, even if it is terrible. It's better to know…"

Shannon touched the patch over her left eye. "Yes, it's better to know."

"Oh, Shannon, I'm so sorry. I didn't mean to remind you of your…of…"

"My injuries," Shannon finished for her cousin.

"It's okay. We have to face life on its terms. That's just the way it is."

"You've been really brave about it all. I often wonder if the reason I don't remember anything before my mother's funeral is because I'm a coward, that I saw something too awful to remember."

"Your father didn't hurt Aunt Bunny," Shannon assured her. "He was a kind, gentle man."

Shannon knew some people thought Uncle Sean had found his wife with another man and killed them both, then made it look like a boating accident.

"He and Grandfather had some rather violent shouting matches during the years after that. I recall those. He was neither kind nor gentle then."

"Fathers and sons," Shannon said, as if that explained the quarrels. "They often have different ideas."

And men and women, she thought later when she was in bed and listening to the wind moan around the eaves. What had Rory been thinking when he'd kissed her as if he'd never let her go?

And what had she been thinking to kiss him back?

The idea of an affair between them was ridiculous at the best of times, and now, in this dark time...

She shook her head, feeling hopelessly entangled in the web of her particular destiny.

Eight more days.

Would fate be kind?

Chapter Five

"How's Mandy liking pre-school?" Shannon asked.

"Loves it," Kate answered. "She somehow has the idea her class exists just to entertain her. She's good at arts and crafts. And Jess and Jeremy taught her the alphabet and to count to a hundred, so she thinks she's ahead of her classmates and tries to instruct them."

Shannon laughed over her newly adopted cousin's escapades. It helped ease the state of her nerves a little. She didn't want to think about the next hour. Kate was driving her to the doctor's office. Soon the bandages would come off. Then...

Breathing deeply, she sought an inner peace to accept the outcome, whatever it might be. Even if she couldn't see straight off, she still might regain her sight later on.

If she didn't, so what? She could still work and support herself. She wasn't helpless. In fact, she'd done quite well at taking care of herself during the nine days she'd spent at the big house. She'd made sandwiches one day for lunch when Megan was late coming in. And she'd only cut herself once, she added wryly.

"Here we are," Kate said.

Shannon opened the car door as soon as Kate shut off the engine. She walked around the front of the car and waited until Kate took her arm before proceeding. They went inside the clinic.

"Hi, Shannon," the receptionist said. She was one of Shannon's oldest friends from school days and the mother of the eight-year-old who had been in the parade. "I think the nurse is ready for you. Yes, here she is now. Go on back."

Shannon felt like a package being delivered as Kate turned her over to the nurse, then followed along behind them while Shannon was weighed and her blood pressure and temperature taken. Kate took charge of her purse and coat.

"Very good," the nurse announced when she finished. She led them to one of the examining rooms along the hall. "The doctor will be with you in a sec."

"There're clouds over the mountains today," Kate

noted. "It's supposed to snow tonight or tomorrow. We're getting a lot more this year than last."

"Yes. The ski resorts must be ecstatic after several winters of little snow."

"I suppose so—"

The door opened, interrupting the idle conversation. Shannon's heart thudded in anticipation and dread.

"Hey," the doctor said. Mitch Burleson was Kate's age and the grandson of Tom, one of the elders of the town who felt it was his place to keep an eye on everyone and tell them what they were doing wrong in their lives.

"Hi, Mitch," Shannon greeted him, her heart under control once more. Sort of. *Breathe,* she reminded herself.

"Let's get on with it," he suggested. "Did you bring some sunglasses? I don't want you to go without them for the next few days, not even in the house."

"Yes, we have them," Kate said.

Shannon detected impatience in her cousin. A sign of tension, unusual for Kate.

"Ready?" Mitch asked her.

Shannon nodded, her mouth as dry as cracker crumbs. She felt scissors slide under the tape that held the gauze in place. Mitch put a hand over the patches to hold them in place until he finished. She felt the gauze fall loose at her temples.

"I thought eye patches had strings that tied behind your head," she said, forcing a lightness in her voice.

"I suppose if you wear one all the time that would be better," Mitch murmured, sounding preoccupied with his task. "Cara, close the blinds and turn off the light. I don't want a shock to her eyes when I take these off."

Shannon hadn't realized the nurse had returned with the doctor. She heard soft footsteps move about the room.

Mitch leaned close. "Don't be alarmed if you see shooting stars or bursts of light. Your eyes have had a shock. Sometimes they react in odd ways when the light hits them again."

"Okay."

He lifted the patches.

Shannon stared, blinked and stared again. Into darkness. Total. Complete. Darkness.

"There aren't any flashes of light," she reported. Her voice didn't quiver, but inside she felt shaky, confused and frightened, the way she'd been after the shooting. She'd been so sure…so sure…

"Okay, I'm going to check your eyes with a light," Mitch warned.

He held her eyelid open on the right eye, then the left. She didn't detect the light.

"Your reactions are normal," he said in satisfaction. "Actually, everything looks good. Where are the sunglasses?"

Kate handed them over. Shannon put them on.

"You can turn on the light and open the blinds," he told the nurse, then spoke to her once more. "You be sure to wear the sunglasses in the house as well as outdoors. Vision can return slowly or suddenly, in one eye or both. There may be sudden pain, as when you step into the sun after being in a dark room. Call if you have any changes in vision, or headaches, that kind of thing.''

''I will,'' she promised.

Blind. The word beat at her, so dark, so final.

No one would want her.

No husband to share pleasures and sorrows, no sweet babies to cuddle, no grandchildren to delight her later years. None of the things that mattered would be hers. A blind person would be too much of a burden...unless someone loved that person very much.

She couldn't think about it now. There were people around. She had to get home, to her room, then...then she could think.

Holding all emotion in, she thanked Mitch for taking care of her while he wrote a prescription for eyedrops to keep her eyes well lubricated. When she and Kate were in the station wagon again, a heavy sigh escaped her before she could suppress it.

''Well,'' she said, forcing a smile, ''I guess I won't need my new glasses for the foreseeable future.''

''Don't give up,'' Kate said quietly.

Shannon put a hand to her temple. The scar was tender to the touch but no longer painful. The physical wounds were healing. Time was supposed to heal all things.

''I'm not,'' she said, far more certain than she felt. ''I realize now that I really had been expecting everything to be normal as soon as the patches came off. Patience, Prudence,'' she admonished herself, using a childhood term their grandmother had often quoted to the girls.

"Right."

Shannon's heart swelled with love. Kate had waited a long time for the miracle of children and a happy marriage in her own life. Now she had a loving husband, a wonderful stepson and a sweet daughter. It would all come right for her, too, Shannon told her doubting heart. It would.

"Lunch?" Kate asked. "Jess is picking up Mandy today."

Shannon swallowed the fear that clogged her throat. She had to face the town sooner or later. "Sure."

Kate parked, came around the vehicle and tucked her arm into Shannon's. "Courage, love," she murmured. "Brad is just going into the café. He's with the manager of the new Wind River Resort. A woman," Kate added gently.

"I'm fine," Shannon assured her relative, her tone cool and calm. She had no expectations from that quarter.

"He's spotted us," Kate murmured. "Such a gentleman. He's holding the door."

"See if you can't close it in his face," Shannon suggested, "preferably on his nose."

Kate choked on laughter.

Shannon knew when they approached the other

couple. She recognized Brad's cologne immediately, and an expensive perfume mingled with it.

"Brad, hello," she said affably. "How are you?"

"Uh, fine. Fine," he repeated as if at a loss for words.

Shannon turned in the direction of the perfume. "Hi. I'm Shannon Bannock, one of the local cops. You're with the new resort up on the river, right?"

"Yes. I'm the manager."

The woman sounded hesitant. She'd probably heard all about her and Brad from the local grapevine.

"Glad to meet you," Shannon said brightly. "I hope you enjoy living in Wind River. It's a wonderful town, friendly and quiet...with only an occasional shoot-out. Right, Brad?"

"Uh, yeah. Well, I see our table is ready. Nice talking to you. I take it that your eyes, that is, that you're not..."

Shannon almost enjoyed his stumbling about, looking for words. He was usually very smooth talking. "It's too soon to tell," she said airily, as if she weren't the least bit concerned. "The bandages just came off today."

"Hi, darlin', our table is over this way," a familiar masculine baritone informed her.

Before she knew what was happening, Rory had taken her hand, dropped an arm around her shoulders and planted a kiss square on her open, surprised mouth.

"Excuse us," he said and led her off, his arm protectively guiding her among the other diners she could hear in the crowded little restaurant. "Here we are. Kate, you sit on that side. Shannon will sit next to me."

He was graciousness itself, helping her with her down jacket and gloves, making sure she was comfortable in the booth, then putting a napkin into her hand and keeping up a steady stream of chatter so that she couldn't think. She frowned, not sure if she was annoyed or grateful.

"I'm glad you could make it. I'd hoped you two would stop in. So, how did it go at the doctor's office?"

There was a moment of silence, then Kate spoke up. "We don't know anything yet."

A warm hand clasped Shannon's. "No sense of light in either eye?" he asked close to her ear.

Shannon drew away a little, confused by his nearness and his lover-like actions. "Not yet."

"Atta girl," he murmured. His lips grazed her temple.

"What are you doing?" she demanded. Didn't she have enough to contend with without him acting the moonstruck lover in front of the whole town?

"Showing that damn lawyer what an ass he is," Rory said, practically nuzzling her ear. "He is, you know. You wouldn't have been happy with him. You have too much fire and spirit for a dull sort like that."

She was astounded at this assertion. "What do you know about what I want in a relationship with a man?" she inquired in an amused tone designed to put him in his place.

"I know you," he announced even more intimately, clearly having no idea of his place.

He laughed, an intimate, sexy sound that sent chills cascading along her spine and warmth spiraling through her body. Heat hit her face. She managed a laugh. "Maybe you just think you do," she suggested loftily.

His laughter rolled over her like a caress. "Even a blind person should be able to see how it is between us," he murmured, "especially after those passionate kisses."

She actually gasped. The effrontery of the man, to bring up the passion, which had been mutual—

"Uh, I'll have a cheeseburger with everything," Kate said hurriedly. There was barely hidden laughter in her voice. "A house salad. And coffee, please."

"The Chinese chicken salad looks good," Rory said to Shannon, again close to her ear. He laid an arm over the back of the banquette, his chest against her shoulder.

"That's what I'll have," she decided. Anything to get him to move away! "Hot tea with nonfat milk."

His chuckle touched her temple in little puffs of warm breath. "I'm having the steak and fries special. I'll share with you. You like fries with ketchup."

"How do you know that?" she asked in annoyance at his presumed knowledge of her and her tastes. Honestly, he could be so maddening!

"I remember you and Megan having a fight over the ketchup bottle one time when you were here with your folks."

She suddenly remembered it, too. She'd been about eight, Megan seven. The bottle had flown out of her hand when she'd jerked back to keep Megan from grabbing it, then it had sailed over two tables, landed in the middle of the next one and splattered all over a matronly lady's bosom. She and Megan had been grounded for a month.

"That was not one of my finer moments."

"But it was funny. I nearly laughed my head off."

"You would."

Kate and Rory chuckled at her disgruntled tone. After a second, she smiled, too. It *had* been funny.

Suddenly the darkness behind her sunglasses didn't seem as dismal as it had been when she'd left the doctor's office. Well after all, she *was* having lunch with the county's most eligible bachelor, the handsomest man in the whole state. And that was something.

She lifted her chin as she recalled Brad and his companion were there. Rory was much more of a "catch" than the stuffy attorney.

"What are you thinking?" Rory asked.

"That all the other women in the room are probably green at this moment." She turned a brilliant smile his way, sending him a challenge with her facetious remark.

Kate tried to cover a whoop of laughter with a cough. Her effort wasn't very successful.

Shannon couldn't help but giggle. Beside her, she heard Rory's amused chuckle. "Are you using me?" he asked. "Maybe for a little payback time?"

She considered. "Yes, I think I am. But you asked for it."

"Yeah?"

"Yes. You're so vain you probably think Kate and I should be honored to be sitting at the same table with you."

"If I did, you've certainly set me straight," he conceded, his tone reflecting nothing but humor. "You Windraven women are hard on a man's ego."

"I've always been told we were the most fascinating and beautiful women around," Kate said airily, joining in the spirit of the moment.

"Oh, you're that, too," he agreed, sending little chills cascading down Shannon's arm where his shoulder touched hers lightly.

During the meal, Shannon laughed and chatted easily with the other two. The earlier despair receded and hope resurfaced. She suddenly, and for no good reason, felt charming and witty.

At one point Rory asked her to tell Megan he'd be out to check the mare that evening. She invited him to join her and Megan and Grandfather for dinner again. He accepted.

Later, as Kate drove her to the ranch, she wondered if that wasn't an odd thing—to learn she still couldn't see, but to have a good time, anyway.

It was something to think about. Maybe to worry about. Because Rory Daniels, the heartthrob of the county, was an enigma in her life, and she didn't need any more alarming situations at the present.

"Here we are. Lunch was fun, wasn't it?" Kate

said as she stopped at the walkway up to the big house. "Rory has always been one of my favorite people."

Shannon paused with her hand on the door handle. "So why didn't you two get together years ago?"

"What? Date an underclassman? Never!" After a moment, she added thoughtfully, "I've frequently wondered about him. With his looks, you'd think some female would've snapped him up long ago."

"Maybe he didn't snap back. It takes two. He may be matrimony-shy for reasons we don't know."

"Yeah, a great unrequited love," Kate finished on a note of sympathetic humor. "Well, I'd better go rescue Jess from Mandy. She loves to give orders, and the fellows indulge her shamelessly."

Shannon waved goodbye and walked up the sidewalk and into the house by herself, finding the two steps without mishap. A simple task, but she felt good at accomplishing it. After hanging up her outdoor clothing, she went into the living room.

Hearing strange noises, she realized her grandfather was asleep in his wheelchair. She quietly took her place in the rocking chair and contemplated the future. Perhaps it was time she moved into her house and really learned to take care of herself. She wouldn't stay here and depend on her cousins to do it for her.

She clasped her hands tightly. To be alone in a house and not be able to see... What if something happened? She tried to imagine what. A fire because she forgot something on the stove? Someone breaking into the house?

The latter was a frightening idea. The fact that the robber who'd shot her was still free didn't help her peace of mind. But she'd lived on her own for nine years. Did she have the courage to try it without sight?

Megan and Rory entered the side door of the kitchen shortly after six that evening. Shannon smiled brightly in that direction. "Dinner is ready," she announced.

"Wow, what service," Megan exclaimed in pleasure. "Did you fix it?"

"With Grandfather's help," she said, placing sliced tomatoes on the salad plates. She was aware that Rory had approached her.

"Smells good," he said a second before cold hands slid into her hair and cupped her neck, causing a chill.

"Beast," she reprimanded, pulling away. "Can you take the salads in to the table? Megan, the chicken is in the oven. I'll bring the veggies."

"Yes. What's this?" he asked. He caught her hands.

She tried to pull away. "Nothing."

"A burn. Two of them. What's under the bandage?"

"A cut. A small one," she added when he continued to hold her hands in his.

His hands were cool as he examined her battle scars, as she dubbed her efforts to prepare a meal. It had been harder than she'd thought. If not for her grandfather, she'd have given up. But she had to learn to do things on her own if she was to be independent.

Retreating, she carefully lifted two bowls, one of hot potato salad, the other of asparagus, and held them out to Rory. "Here. Make yourself useful."

He took the bowls. She felt his body heat as he moved beside her, his shirt brushing her arm.

"You shouldn't have gone to such trouble," Megan told her in a worried voice.

"I wanted to practice." She turned toward Megan. "I think it's time I moved to my house."

"Oh, but you can't—" Megan began.

"I think that's an excellent idea," Rory said smoothly. "Didn't you say you had a paper to write?"

"Yes." Shannon had thought it out that afternoon. "I need to finish the dissertation, then I can start my family-counseling clinic. It's been my dream for years."

"Go for it," he advised.

Shannon heard the soft hum of the wheelchair motor. "She needs...to stay here," her grandfather said, moving toward the dining room.

In the tense silence that followed, Shannon could imagine Megan and Grandfather frowning at their guest while he challenged them with a sardonic smile and a dare in those challenging blue eyes.

She suddenly recalled the shoot-out. When she'd opened her eyes after being shot, when her guardian angel had lifted her, she'd seen an explosion of light that had shrunk down to twin spots of intense blue. Could she have been looking into Rory's eyes at that moment?

But no. That was after she'd been shot. Her vision was already gone.

But what if it wasn't?

Excitement rippled through her. Had she been able to see, if only for a brief second, after being injured? If so…if so… There was a world of promise in the idea.

"What are you thinking?" Rory asked.

She wasn't ready to divulge the hope that wouldn't quite go away. "We'd better eat before it gets cold. There's barbecued chicken in the oven," she told them. "If someone would please get it out. I've already fought with the oven twice tonight. It's ahead, two to zero," she said, referring lightly to the burns she'd sustained earlier.

They talked of ranch business for the next hour. Shannon accepted compliments on her cooking from the other three with a taut smile. She was very tired, she realized, pushing the dark glasses up her nose.

"I'll clean the kitchen," she said decisively when they finished, knowing she needed to show her family she could make it on her own.

"I'll carry the dishes in," Rory volunteered. "You put them in the dishwasher. Meg, you've had a full day. You rest. Add a log to the fire."

Shannon sensed Megan's uncertainty in the tiny pause that followed Rory's orders before she acceded. When she and Grandfather vacated the dining room,

Shannon gathered a stack of plates. Across from her, she could hear Rory doing the same. He followed her into the kitchen.

"Stick to your guns," he said after bringing in the last of the dishes.

She rinsed plates and silverware and placed them gently in the dishwasher. "What do you mean?"

"Move into your house."

"Oh. Yes, I intend to."

He chuckled. "You'll be next door to me," he said in a sexy tone.

"Well, across the creek," she corrected. "It must be a couple of hundred feet between the houses. With the woods and creek between, we won't intrude on each other."

"I was thinking of building a bridge over the creek."

She was startled at how much she liked the idea. "Why?"

"To be neighborly. It'll make it easier for us to run back and forth. I won't have to worry about you falling on a slippery rock and drowning."

"I'd hardly drown. The creek isn't more than two feet deep during spring snowmelt."

"I'd worry, anyway."

Since there was laughter in his voice, she wasn't sure how to take him. She opted for a stern note. "Besides, why should we run back and forth? We'll each be busy with our own lives."

"I thought I could help you with your research

notes and you could repay me with home-cooked meals. The way to a man's heart and all that.''

She shut the dishwasher door with a startled slam. ''I'm not looking for the way to any man's heart,'' she declared with an indignant frown.

''We're pretending to be lovers, remember?''

''We most certainly are not!''

He was suddenly close, very close. ''We can make it real.''

Before she could come up with a quelling reply, he'd gathered her into his arms.

''The dishes—''

''Are done,'' he finished. ''I wiped the counter and the stove. Everything is neat. Now don't I get a reward?''

His warmth engulfed her senses. She wanted his kiss, she realized. Very, very much. Her blood seemed to thicken so that her heart had to beat very hard to send it through her body.

''No,'' she whispered.

''No?''

''I...we shouldn't.''

''Why?''

His nose touched hers. She instinctively tilted her head to one side. ''Because.'' She couldn't think of a good reason, other than the whole idea of her and him was...was ridiculous. ''It's ridiculous,'' she said, grabbing the word like a lifeline.

''Maybe, but consider this—I want to make love to you. I think you want it, too.''

The words caused a place inside her to ache. "I—I didn't think...I wasn't sure anyone would want—"

She stopped before she bared the horrible uncertainty she felt. She didn't want his pity.

"...someone as beautiful as you?" he finished for her. "You turn me on, lady cop. You know that, don't you?"

His words shook her composure. She couldn't think beyond the memory of his lips on hers. And she couldn't stand being apart another second.

Stretching upward only an inch, she encountered his lips. Their mouths meshed hungrily, and she felt the need, his as well as hers. Hunger consumed her like fire.

When he shifted slightly, she found herself securely enclosed, the counter behind her, his arms forming a triangle as he gripped the edge with his hands. Only his mouth touched her, but she was vitally aware of the rest of his tall, manly frame an inch away. She had only to press forward the least bit...

She didn't.

"Kiss me back," he ordered in a low growl when she valiantly stopped her wild response. "I need your mouth."

"Rory—"

"Don't argue."

She tried to think. One of them had to. "This isn't wise. Don't you understand? I'm...I'm..." She couldn't quite bring herself to say the dreaded word aloud. "I may never see—"

"Shut up and kiss me."

When she lifted her hands to his chest, intending to gently push him away until he regained his senses, she realized her mistake immediately. She flattened her palms against him and absorbed his wonderful warmth and the hard masculine feel of him right down to her toes.

For the first time in her life she wanted mind-blowing. She wanted unthinking passion. She wanted fulfillment.

"No," she whispered. "No, no, no."

"Yes," he said, just as fierce.

But he lifted his head and stood there without moving for the longest time, for an eternity of pounding heartbeats and contrary yearning. She knew he was staring down at her, his gaze so intent, she could feel it.

"Why?" he murmured on a hoarse note. "Why not?"

She shook her head, not knowing what the answer was. She didn't even know the question.

When he took a deep breath, she felt his shirt brush against her breasts. They hardened into tiny aching points at once. She shook her head again, confused by this strange rapture that took hold of her whenever they touched.

"It's so odd," she said, voicing the confusion that gripped both of them.

He stepped back and cold air rushed in where he had been. The longing rose from someplace deep inside, telling her to quit resisting something so wonderful.

"What's so strange? A man and a woman who want each other? Hardly," he scoffed, but in an oddly gentle way. "Haven't you ever wanted like this before?"

"No," she said, shocked at even the thought of being so out of control. Until the shoot-out, her life had been serene. Sensible. Planned.

His hand touched her temple. "Then you have a lot to learn, Officer Bannock," he teased, but with a deeply serious inflection running through the words.

It caused a shiver to chase over her nerves again. She drew away.

"Shall I come by for you tomorrow at noon?" Rory asked before she thought of a retort.

The shift in subject threw her off-balance. "What for?"

"To take you home. Megan is going to the Thoroughbred auction. I assumed you wouldn't be foolish enough to try to walk three miles on a frozen road."

"Kate—"

"She has a family to take care of. You can't expect her to be at your disposal all the time."

"I don't," she said in annoyance. "You twist my meaning every time I try to say something."

"Sorry. Do you want a ride or not?"

Ignoring his impatience, she considered. "All right, I'll accept your gracious offer." She gave him a sarcastic smile as she got the last word in.

"Good. See you then. Thanks for dinner. It was delicious."

After he walked out, Shannon stood there as if still

trapped against the counter. Somehow...somehow she felt he'd gotten his way, after all.

It wasn't until she was in bed that she remembered she would be alone in the new house. But everything would be okay, she reassured her flagging spirits. She could do it.

Chapter Six

With one hand on her grandfather's wheelchair, Shannon lifted her face skyward as she stepped out on the south terrace. "The sun feels so bright and warm," she murmured.

When the wheelchair stopped, she stood there for a moment, basking in the fresh morning air, before finding the patio table, then the bench beside it. Taking a seat, she sighed deeply and rested her elbows on the tabletop. She and her grandfather were alone. Megan was at the auction, looking over the mares for brood stock.

"Living in town, I forgot how quiet the ranch can be. It reaches clear to the soul," Shannon continued.

Her grandfather snorted, which she took for agreement. She studied the sounds around them—the far-away squeal of playful yearlings in the pasture, the soft moo of a cow calling her calf to her, the twitter of birds coming from the trees near the stable.

The ache of some unknown emotion soaked through her, hurting her in places she didn't know existed. She couldn't define the pain or where it came from.

Nostalgia?

Perhaps, but for what? What elusive thing of the past called to her with bittersweet need and made her sigh in longing for that which she couldn't name?

"There are no words," she said softly, regretfully, voicing the thought, unable to stifle the sweep of yearning that went right to the center of her being. Once she had wanted so much, had planned and worked toward her goals, and now there was this terrible insecurity about the future.

A crow cawed, its rough voice malcontent, disturbing the gentler tenor of the morning.

"The ravens," she said, recalling the Windraven legend of the ravens' warning before a disaster struck. "What more can happen to our family?"

Not even the wind answered the philosophical question. A soft snore told her that Grandfather was asleep.

She sighed again and wondered how he had stood his pain so valiantly all these years. Crippled. Nearly silent. His thoughts scrambled as he searched for words he'd long known but couldn't recall. He'd faced it all without complaint.

"Sometimes I want to scream and rant, to wail at the unfairness of it all," she said in a whisper. Tears gathered at the back of her throat. She fought them off. "And sometimes...sometimes I have cried."

Not only for the loss of her sight, but for the hopes she'd nourished, for all the things that had seemed good and true but were turning out differently.

The crow cawed morosely, closer this time.

"Disaster draws near." The hair prickled at the back of her neck. "The Windraven legacy."

It seemed to her it was a legacy of disappointment and deep pain. Regret. Unfilled hunger that plagued the spirit. Lost love. Forgotten dreams.

An odd sound caught her attention. She listened intently. Her grandfather sniffed again. She realized he wasn't sleeping.

She touched his arm. He caught her hand in his, his grip shockingly weak. Liquid warmth struck her hand and ran along the back, swiftly cooling in the January air.

Guilt replaced the odd nostalgia. Some comfort she was, whining when he'd been in a wheelchair for years with never a show of self-pity. "I'm sorry," she said. "I didn't mean to upset you."

"Not...you," he said in a raw tone. "Life. Old mistakes. Can't...undo."

She stroked the back of his hand and suppressed her own tears. "I know. A person can't go back. We can't reset the clock and make things happen the way they should have. I remember when Uncle Sean died, how awful it was."

''My last.''

''Yes, all your children gone before you,'' she said, choking on the thought of his loneliness and grief. ''My mother once said the Windom inheritance was misery and misfortune.''

''Human. To err.''

''To err is human—to forgive, divine?''

He made a sound which she took for assent.

She wondered about him and his first love. Had someone come between them, made them distrust each other? Was that why his fiancée had gone to another man and married him a month before the wedding date with Grandfather?

Tears filled her eyes. It was all so sad. ''Humans. We make ourselves miserable.''

The patio door opened at the same time as she heard a truck on the road. ''Dr. Daniels is here,'' Mrs. Roddey said, approaching the table.

Her husband and son leased the ranch pastures and raised beef cattle during the summer. In the fall they sold off the calves and fed only the breeding herd during the winter. The wife helped out at the ranch whenever they needed someone.

''So I hear.'' Shannon recognized his truck easily now.

''I'm leaving in a minute. I've fixed a bite of lunch. Is Dr. Daniels going to eat with you?'' Mrs. Roddey asked.

''I suppose.'' Shannon wasn't sure she wanted to see him just now. Her spirits were low today. She didn't feel up to his teasing, sensual play.

"I'll go get a plate for him then."

Shannon nodded, intensely aware of many things all at once. Inhaling deeply, she detected cinnamon rolls over the aroma of beef stew. She heard Mrs. Roddey bustle out after setting a tray on the table. A slammed truck door, then booted footsteps on the patio steps told her when Rory arrived.

"Hello," she said, turning in that direction.

"Hello yourself."

His voice was husky, as seductive as warm cocoa going down and warming your insides on a cold night. A tremor raced through her. Feeling as if every nerve was exposed, she gestured toward the tray, intending to invite him to join them, and hit a cup. "Oh," she murmured, hearing the clatter of glass and the splash of liquid.

A hand caught hers and pulled it back when she would have explored to find out what she'd done.

"Careful. That's hot," he advised.

"What did I do?" she asked ruefully, angry with herself for letting nerves overcome sense.

"Spilled a little tea. No harm done. It went on the saucer, a bit on the tray." He sniffed. "That smells good. Got enough for one more?"

"Yes. Mrs. Roddey's bringing you a plate."

"Good. Hello, Mr. Windom. Nice weather we're having today for a change. Shall I move this bench so you can get to the table?"

Her grandfather must have indicated agreement. She heard the bench on the opposite side being shifted. The next thing she was aware of, Rory was sliding onto her bench, his hip touching hers as he swung his long legs over the edge. He spoke to Mrs. Roddey when she returned, then served Shannon and presumably her grandfather and himself, to judge by the sounds and his comments.

"Eat," he encouraged. "This stew is delicious."

She picked up her spoon after laying a napkin in her lap. Self-conscious, she began to eat, knowing if she moved a quarter inch their hips might brush. She held herself perfectly still until he began to speak.

He told of his morning and the patients he'd seen. He spoke of his worries concerning the horse Megan was training for the rich dude. "If he goes vicious and hurts someone, he'll have to be put down. Megan thinks there is a real possibility of that."

"Too much…"

Rory waited patiently for her grandfather to find the word.

"Inbreeding," the older man finished.

"Yes, I'm afraid you're right about this one. All the worst qualities of the breed are coming out in him, but he's a beauty as far as conformation and coloring go."

Shannon felt him turn to her. He described the horse in detail, down to the white stockings on all four feet, the star on its forehead and the length of its tail.

"A lot of folks don't realize how important a tail is to a horse," he concluded.

Shannon burst out laughing, surprising herself. She finished the meal and carefully wiped her mouth.

Beside her, Rory chuckled dryly. "Sorry, didn't mean to get carried away and lecture you."

"That's okay."

"Are you ready to go home?"

Terror grabbed hold of her. "Yes."

"Don't be afraid. I'll be right next door."

Lifting her chin, she informed him she wasn't at all afraid and would be fine.

"Good girl. Mr. Windom, are you ready to go in? I think I need to get home and have a nap. I was up until two this morning over at the Herriot place. Their prize mare took sick."

Shannon wasn't sure if she was irritated or not as Rory took over, ushering her grandfather into the house and her out to his truck, carrying her large bag, the toiletry case tucked under an arm, while he guided her with the other hand. She gripped her purse while he fastened the seat belt across her lap, his hands almost but not quite intimate as he worked. At last they were on their way.

"Home," he said a few minutes later, stopping the truck after a short drive that was over way too soon.

She again felt the clutch of fear and had to battle it. She could do this. She could make it on her own. Other people adjusted and learned. She would, too.

"I'll have to get a dog," she said brightly, hopping out of the truck and heading for the door.

A hand gripped her arm. "Whoa. That's the wrong way."

She turned, needing to be alone, to grow used to this uncertainty. Her eyes burned. Moving blindly and too fast, she banged into him and hit his chin with her head in her rush to get into the house before she cried or did something equally stupid. "Sorry," she said stiffly, stepping back and tripping over a stone.

Capable hands steadied her as she rocked backwards. "Don't," he murmured as if he understood, his voice deep and very close.

Using anger as a crutch to cover other emotions—such as the fear that overshadowed all else—she waited. "If you'll point me toward the front door, I'm sure I'll be fine."

"Maybe *you* will," he muttered, moving back.

She heard him shuffle the suitcases, then take her arm again. Seething with a tangle of feelings she couldn't name, she allowed him to show her the way to her new home, a place that felt as unfamiliar as a hotel in a strange city, even though she'd done most of the remodeling on her free days.

One thing at a time, she reminded herself. One thing— "Oh!" she said as she tripped again.

"Sorry, forgot to mention the step."

He, too, sounded angry. Holding on to her poise with an effort, she found the knob and turned it. Relieved to discover it open—since she couldn't remember where the key was—she led the way inside, envisioning the layout as she went. She felt on firmer ground as she found the kitchen counter and laid her purse on it.

"Thank you for bringing me home. Just put the luggage anywhere. I'll take it to the bedroom later."

She realized she sounded about as grateful as a hoodlum thanking a cop for being arrested.

"What's your problem?" Rory demanded, needled by her polite and totally insincere thanks.

Obviously she was irritated with him. It was too much after the night and morning he'd put in. He'd also gone to great trouble to rearrange his schedule so he could pick her up. So much for gratitude. He was irritated, too.

And he couldn't for the life of him figure out why.

"Not a thing," she replied in a prissy way that drove him to fury. He wanted to kiss the polite smile off her face, then walk out, leaving her breathless and disheveled and restless.

The way he was restless?

Yeah.

Shaking his head, he tried to figure out what the hell was wrong with *him*. Considering the state of his libido, he could easily identify one problem he had.

"Which bedroom?" he asked, his jaw clenched so tight he could hardly speak.

"The back one." She touched the wall, oriented herself, then pointed down the hall.

He headed that way, aware that she was right behind him. He slowed his pace so she could keep up. The bedroom was the last door on the right. He took in the antique brass bed, the white wicker dresser along one wall and a matching settee, covered with colorful cushions, in front of the double windows at the side of the house.

Putting the two cases on the rose-printed bedspread, he glanced outside. He could see his house through the small grove of cottonwoods that lined the creek. It was much closer than he'd realized. His bedroom window faced the creek, too. He could look straight across to hers.

Sweat broke out on his upper lip while heat gathered deep in his body. He suddenly wished he hadn't insisted on being such a thoughtful neighbor.

Because he now had a hunger for a blind woman and it somehow seemed ungentlemanly to give in to it in her present condition?

Yeah, you got it, he told his conscience. She was too vulnerable at present.... He paused and considered when, in the foreseeable future, she might not be.

"Well, thanks," Shannon said behind him.

A dismissal. He swung around and faced her. Standing with her weight on one foot as if she might bolt at any moment, she was particularly beautiful in the soft light.

"Let's do a tour of the house," he suggested. For reasons he couldn't begin to fathom, he refused to let her heave him out the door. "I'll help you with your cases."

"I can manage."

The polite smile was gone. Grinning when she turned a severe frown on him, he realized he felt much better at the honest anger. He didn't want to be treated as politely as a stranger. He was her friend, if she only realized it.

Was that the only reason?

He really wished the annoying inner voice would

go away. It wasn't as if he meant to take advantage of her or the awareness between them.

Pausing, he considered. Well, he didn't mean to when he was thinking clearly. She was emotionally at risk until she got her confidence back. He wanted her to come to him as an equal. Not in gratitude. Not in fear. Only in passion.

Passion. He cursed mentally at the reaction of his body when he thought of sharing that most elemental of human endeavors with this woman.

"Okay," he said, stopping in front of her, wishing he could see her eyes clearly behind the dark glasses. "I'll keep my distance. For now. You need a chance to learn your own capabilities without the added confusion of this thing between us."

She huffed indignantly. "There is nothing between us."

"Don't kid yourself."

Reaching out, he touched her cheek, then slid his hand into the warm strands of red-gold and dark honey waves. She caught her breath and held it for a fifteen-second count before releasing it abruptly.

"See?" he said, pleased with her reaction...until he realized his own breath was jerky.

She pushed his hand away. He struggled with an urge to show her just how strong the attraction was between them. He had a feeling she'd never run into this before.

Neither had he. Along with the need, he felt a host of other, less easily defined emotions. Pity? Maybe.

A need to protect and succor? Sort of. Concern? Yeah.

However, just because he was the first on the scene didn't make him responsible for her. She wouldn't take pity or charity from anyone. That's why he'd encouraged her to come home. She didn't need to have her relatives waiting on her, making her into an invalid before she had a chance to learn her own strengths.

A picture of her in her uniform, directing traffic, the world at her command, came to him. He wanted to see that woman again—the beautiful lady cop who could handle any calamity. And he would. No matter what it took to get her there.

After muttering a disgruntled goodbye, he left the cheerful ranch house with its pale cream walls and sage green woodwork. Crossing the creek via the bridge foundation of four by fours he'd laid down yesterday, he thought of the work needed on the house where he now lived. It could use a woman's delicate touch and eye for color.

The librarian he'd decided on?

He couldn't stop the sardonic snort of amusement. Right. As soon as he got Shannon Bannock out of his system, he'd start looking for his dream woman.

Sobering, he wondered exactly what it would take to eradicate the lady cop from his thoughts. He was pretty sure he knew the answer to that. No way was he going to get mixed up with her, however. She was too vulnerable at the present.

His chest tightened as he thought of her courage,

so much greater than she thought. Yeah, above all else he wanted to play fair with her.

Shannon listened to the echoing silence after the back door closed with a moderate slam that indicated control as well as temper. Frowning, she had to admit she didn't understand the pulsating awareness between her and her confusing neighbor.

Desire.

He'd been right about that; it was something new to her. She'd never encountered a force that drove out all sense of self-preservation, that made her want to cling and touch and kiss and demand...

Pressing a hand to her temple, she automatically checked the short hair there and the tenderness of the scar tissue beneath. She thought this mad longing must somehow be the result of the injury, that being hurt had somehow made her more susceptible and less in control of her emotions and the passion that flooded through her when he was near.

Otherwise, why did she feel it now and not with Brad when he had kissed her?

Touching her lips and recalling the fierce delight of Rory's mouth, she wondered at his sudden passion. Again, it had to be connected to the incident, to his compassion and sense of responsibility because of her injury.

She swallowed against the hard knot of misery that grew in her chest. She didn't want pity. She wanted... She didn't know what she wanted.

Only a couple of weeks ago, she'd been thinking

of home and hearth and a husband to share them with her. Now...now she saw only loneliness down the long, dark road of the future. Who would want to share life with her?

Not Brad, came the answer from some harder, more caustic part of her than she'd known existed. And no other man in his right mind.

An image of Rory as he'd been the night of the parade came to her. A warm feeling invaded her. He had asked her out for hot chocolate. So maybe the interest had been kindled at that moment, and during this past two weeks he'd realized it had grown to a blazing, uncontrollable passion.

Right.

She laughed, not very merrily, but still, a laugh. It helped overcome the daunting silence of her new home and the helplessness she'd felt upon arriving.

Holding both hands out cautiously, she began to explore the place. At the bed, she removed her clothing from the big suitcase and put it away without too much difficulty. She'd kept the same items in the same drawers since she'd lived on her own. The closet was a walk-in just as her old one had been, and the clothes she'd already moved were in it and in the usual order. She found she could recognize most pieces by their cut and feel. She stored the items from her toiletry case in the bathroom, again going by memory.

Exploring the rest of the room, she found English ivy growing in a pot on a table. The table was beside the wicker love seat. Feeling warmth on her hand, she touched the window.

The glass was cold, a contrast to the sunlight streaming through the pane. She pictured the lawn and the mountains, the little creek with its line of trees, the house across the way where Rory lived.

Shying from the latter scene, she went from room to room of her new home, reviving her memory of furniture and pictures and color in the living room, the old-fashioned butler's pantry that she intended to use for an office, and the guest bedroom with its tapestry print wallpaper and brass-accented fireplace. She returned to the kitchen.

After exploring the refrigerator and finding it bare except for condiment bottles and pickles and such, she took a seat at the table. She didn't know what to do next.

Outside a bird chirped shrilly. Inside there was silence.

She removed her sunglasses and rubbed her eyes. Slowly she turned her head this way and that, trying to discern a shadow, the bulky outline of the refrigerator or a slight flicker of light that might indicate a window.

Nothing.

She inhaled slowly and recalled all the reassurances of the doctor and her cousins. It wasn't hopeless. She might see again. Or she might not.

With no one there to witness her lapse, she found it was harder to put up a smiling front. Laying her arms on the table and using them as a pillow, she hid her face and finally let the uncertainty overtake her.

She wept for the fantasies she'd held dear as a child. She wept for the dreams she'd harbored in her heart, the fragile ones that had stubbornly refused to die. And last, she wept for a future that was never meant to be as she finally let the dreams go.

When the useless tears were gone, she pushed herself upright and slipped the dark glasses back in place. She would find new dreams, better ones, and start her life over, she vowed. She blew her nose and decided it was time to prepare a meal.

Finding a ham bone in the freezer, she set it to stewing with bay leaves, garlic and pepper. She'd make soup for supper. Maybe it wasn't a lot, but it was a beginning. She smiled ruefully. Today, the soup; tomorrow...

She'd let tomorrow take care of itself.

Chapter Seven

The first thing Rory did that evening upon arriving at his house was check the house next door. It was dark.

A blind person hardly had need for light, he reminded himself. But it still bothered him. A home should be lit up at night, if only to let burglars know the family was in.

He showered and dressed in a pair of navy sweats and warm socks, then stood at the bedroom window and watched Shannon's place for any signs of movement.

Nothing. Not a shadow at any window. The house looked deserted. A blatant invitation to a vagrant looking for an easy break-in and a bed for the night.

Worry gnawed at his conscience. He tried to ignore it while he heated up a can of soup and made a sandwich. He hesitated, then made two sandwiches.

Disgusted with himself, he pulled on shoes and a coat, slapped the two sandwiches on a plate, grabbed a carton of milk and headed across the backyard. At Shannon's back door, he knocked, then went inside.

"Shannon," he yelled.

"What?"

Her startled voice was so close it startled him. She stood at the sink, the faint light in the western sky outlining her upper body like a silver aura.

"It's me," he announced. "I brought you some supper."

"Why?"

He flipped on the overhead light. "It occurred to me you might be hungry," he said sarcastically.

She gestured toward the stove, her chin tilted at a haughty angle. "I made a pot of soup."

"Well, I brought some milk." He set his obviously unnecessary offerings on the table. "And a couple of grilled cheese sandwiches." The meal looked pretty meager.

"Megan brought milk and bread and fresh vegetables when she returned from the auction," Shannon said, dismissing his efforts with cool disdain.

He frowned, perversely irritated with her for being so damn self-sufficient when earlier he'd thought it best for her to get away from her cousin's home and be on her own. He recalled another grievance.

"There wasn't a light on in the house when I got home."

Her eyebrows, dark brown arches shaped like gull's wings, rose in tandem. "Am I supposed to go over and light the home fires for you?"

"Hardly. I meant *your* lights weren't on."

She turned toward the window. "Is it dark already?"

"Yes."

"Oh." She put a hand to her dark glasses. "It's odd, not to know day from night. How do you think a person learns to tell the difference?"

As worry knitted twin lines between her eyes, his anger underwent a sudden change. Instinctively he closed the three steps between them and took her in his arms. "I don't know."

She backed from his embrace, her hands in front, palms out, as if to hold him off. He stopped.

Spying the mantel clock across the hall, he said, "You have a clock in the living room. Doesn't it chime?"

"It used to. I turned it off because it woke me up during the day when I was working night shift."

"I'll check it."

He flicked on the lamp in the living room and opened the glass face of the clock. He found a key inside and a lever that switched off the chime mechanism. In a moment, he had it ticking merrily. Four tones rang out the half hour.

"There, it's working," he said when he saw her standing in the doorway, her face turned toward him as if she were observing his every movement, her manner pensive.

He smiled, then recalled she couldn't see it. It occurred to him that for once in his life he couldn't use the half-smile and oblique glance that worked like a charm on women of all ages—he'd used it to get past the dragon at the desk in the hospital—on this woman.

Her head titled slightly to the side. "Would you like a bowl of soup?" she inquired politely. "It's a sort of made-up recipe with ham and mixed vegetables and tomatoes and kidney beans. I opened the beans when I was searching for the canned tomatoes. Fresh or frozen stuff I can identify by shape, but cans..." She shrugged.

"I can see how that would be a problem. The soup smells great. Sure beats the tomato soup I was going to have."

Her smile was quick and surprisingly warm. "Grilled cheese sandwiches and tomato soup? Comfort food. My mother used to fix that when I had a sore throat."

He took her hand and tucked it in the crook of his arm. "Dinner awaits, madam. Shall we dine?"

"I'd be honored, I'm sure."

Sticking her nose in the air like some blue-blooded society matron, she let him escort her to the table. He served the soup, then poured milk and got out spoons and napkins. Done, he sat opposite her.

The sky darkened to obsidian while they ate. He chatted about his cases and his worry over the mare at the Herriot ranch. During a pause, he felt the peace of the house descend on him. Observing Shannon as she carefully wiped her mouth, he wished *she* was his quiet, safe librarian.

An odd thought, that. Shannon Bannock, with her vivid passion and independent attitude, was anything but safe, in his opinion. But she was lovely. And desirable.

His body kept reminding him of that little fact every so often. A gentleman wouldn't take advantage of her at this difficult point in her life, but when she regained her sight, it might be a different story between them. Maybe then he wouldn't go home after dinner but would spend the night locked in sweet dreams with her.

"I'll bring over a couple of timers for your lamps and set them to turn on at five and off at ten. That way," he added before she could protest, "no one will think the house is empty and decide to move in."

"Oh," she said, her lips pursing in an enticing way. "I didn't think about that. Thank you for mentioning it."

"You should keep your doors locked, too."

"Okay."

Surprised at her quick acquiescence, he left. At home, he puzzled over his equal parts attraction and irritation with her, then laughed at his own confusion. He wasn't a boy caught in the throes of his first love. He understood male-female interest quite well. Where Shannon was concerned, the feeling was very strong indeed.

* * *

Shannon heard the mantel clock strike six. She yawned and stretched, feeling surprisingly refreshed. After dinner with her sexy, surly neighbor last night, she'd forced herself to go to bed after the ten o'clock news. She was determined to keep "normal" waking and sleeping hours.

Having made it through half a day and an evening on her own, she felt capable and in control once more.

After she showered and dressed, she fixed a bowl of cereal. Remembering Rory's admonition, she flicked on the light with a "there, I hope you're satisfied" glance in the direction of his house before she sat down to eat.

She wondered if he was up yet. And if he slept in anything. His skivvies? Pajama bottoms? Bare skin?

Disturbed by the images this produced, her errant thoughts nevertheless veered off to contemplation of sleeping with him, of waking in his arms, snug in their warm bed on cold mornings. It sounded... heavenly.

She'd had a steady in college, but then she'd gotten more and more involved in her studies and spent less and less time with him. When he'd pressed for commitment, it had been she who had backed away.

With Brad, she'd thought there was a possibility. Now she realized she hadn't felt strongly enough about him to include him in her plans. From her psychology courses, she knew herself well enough to realize she would have to trust a man a great deal to share her heart and thus her body. But no man had ever made her want to go that final step.

Except Rory Daniels.

She frowned. There was this sensual thing between them, but neither she nor Rory would let it get out of hand.

Besides, no man would want to get too deeply involved with someone like her, someone who possibly would be a handicap all her life.

Leaping to her feet, she got busy. After washing and drying the dishes, she decided to dust the house. She nearly broke a lamp and a glass butterfly, but she managed.

After that, she scrubbed the bathroom. Then she set out a few more knickknacks stored in a drawer of the breakfront that had been her mother's. Even if she couldn't see them, others could. She wanted her home to be pleasant.

The telephone rang as she was trying to think what to do next. Having time on her hands wasn't a thing she was used to. She spoke to a friend about the state of the town. People were still upset that the robber was on the loose. The sheriff thought the man was long gone from these parts. A new deputy had been hired in her place. After they hung up, Shannon wondered if the man knew how to handle domestic problems.

Thinking about domestic problems made her think about her father. He hadn't been able to stick it out. Uncle Sean and Aunt Bunny had been madly in love and yet there had been something wrong in their marriage.

She was thankful when the telephone rang again, interrupting her unsettling thoughts. She talked to another friend, then another, then the sheriff. Finally Kate's husband, Jess, called. He had nothing new on her case.

After lunch, she took a nap on the sofa with the sounds of Debussy's La Mer lulling her to sleep. Later, restless again, she dressed warmly and ventured outside.

Guilt niggled at her as she opened the back door. She'd forgotten to lock it last night. Rory had, too, when he'd left.

Inhaling the pure cold air, she stepped carefully off the concrete porch onto the grass. Earlier, the weatherman had said snow was predicted. She loved to watch the flakes float down from the sky. As a kid, she'd thought it magical.

A sigh pushed its way out of her. She wasn't a kid. She had to face life as it was. If there was a fifty percent chance she might see again, there was also a fifty percent chance that she wouldn't. Those were the facts.

She walked a few feet from the porch, keeping to a straight line. When she reached the line of trees that marked the woods, she would turn back. Her hands out, she pressed forward, forcing herself past the fear that slowed her steps. She had to get used to being alone.

* * *

Rory parked, went into his house and straight out the back. Megan had mentioned she'd gotten no answer at Shannon's when she'd called earlier. Standing on the deck, he studied the rock-and-timber house next door.

She'd had it painted during a warm spell in the late fall. The bathroom had new fixtures, as did the old-fashioned kitchen. With plants and pictures of gardens, the house had a friendly air. Welcoming. But maybe not to him.

With a rueful grimace, he crossed the four by fours over the creek and stopped at her back door. No lights shone inside. The door wasn't locked. He went in.

He knew no one was home before he glanced into every room. Where the hell was she?

An afghan was flung carelessly over the back of the sofa. A cushion showed the imprint of a head at one end. She'd lain there at some time. Probably when Megan had been trying to reach her. But where was she now?

The hair rose on the back of his neck as he was forced to consider the possibilities. Surely she wouldn't be stupid enough to go outside. People had been lost in these woods, hunters who thought they knew the area.

His insides went cold. Grimly he went out and surveyed the yard, then walked around the house. Returning to the backyard, he studied the ground. Shannon was tall, but slight. Her weight wouldn't make much of an impression in the dry stubble. Finally he spotted a footprint.

He found a definite track in the dust at the edge of the woods. His heart thudded loudly, sounding like a bass drum ringing in his ears. The shoe imprint was small and slender, and it was fresh.

"Shannon," he called as loudly as he could. He listened but heard only the sound of the wind as it rushed down the mountains. A storm was blowing in from the west.

He called again, a sense of urgency driving him. The only answer was the cry of a crow by the creek. By heavens, he would take a strip off her hide when he found her.

He tried not to think about his part in encouraging her to leave her grandfather's house and strike out on her own. If something happened, if she was hurt...

Driven by mounting anxiety, he tried to pick up a trail in the woods. Failing that, he walked in a broad zigzag.

"Shannon!" he yelled and felt the first snowflake land gently on his eyelash. The storm had arrived.

Shannon ran headlong into a tree. Startled, she put a mittened hand on the rough bark and one to her forehead. She'd have a bruise there, darn it. Her nosy neighbor would grill her about it. She turned back toward the house.

And promptly ran into another tree.

Puzzled, her head smarting, she turned again, but encountered another hard trunk. She pivoted, her hands searching for the open space that should have been there. She found a group of saplings. She turned again. Again there were trees in front of her.

Suddenly all she could hear was the sound of her heart pounding in her ears and the howl of the wind, rustling through the pine needles. She realized she was in the woods, surrounded by trees, with no idea where the house lay.

"Think," she told herself. Her voice was caught and carried away on the wind. The solitude of the woods closed around her, making her feel terribly *alone*.

Sitting on a log, she removed a mitten and held up her hand. If she could tell in which direction the sun lay, she'd know she was west—at least she *thought* so—of the house. She would walk with the sun at her back and find the house or at least the road and thus ascertain her whereabouts.

A bit of cold landed gently on her palm.

Snow.

Her heart lurched. No one knew where she was, including herself. She almost laughed at the irony, but the situation had become too dangerous. With the sun behind the clouds, her hope of finding her own way faltered badly.

Listening, she heard only the softly sibilant ping of the snow on the fallen leaves and the wind ruffling the tree tops. The temperature was dropping.

Pulling her mitten back on, she took a few steps forward. No, no, that wasn't the way. She faced the wind, which was probably coming from the west, then turned her back to it and went a few steps before touching a tree.

The woods had suddenly grown thick and menacing, closing in on her on all sides. She pushed on, trying to keep the wind at her back and her mind functioning, sometimes fighting her way through branches and vines. The snow hit her face in hard little pellets.

After a long time she rested against a sturdy pine, her side aching. She hated that her disappearance would frighten and worry her cousins. They would try to keep it from her grandfather unless it became impossible not to…as in attending her funeral. She pushed on.

A thorn caught around her ankle, digging painfully into the skin and she went down hard. Breathing heavily, she lay there in a bed of leaves, the briars biting into her flesh.

Suddenly it seemed easier to stay there, just not to get up. She was too tired.

She heard a sound, a faint voice in the wind. Her imagination? The sound came again. She sat up.

"Hello," she called. "Hello-o-o."

"Shannon," a voice yelled back.

Startled, she turned her head from side to side, trying to figure where it came from. "Yes. Hello," she shouted.

"Keep calling."

"Hello," she called at three-second intervals. After a period that felt like eternity but was probably only a few minutes or so, she yelled, "Can you hear me?"

"Yes. Keep calling. It's Rory."

"Well, I knew that," she muttered. Relief rushed over her, displacing the odd blankness of a few minutes ago. Energy flooded back into her muscles.

"I can't hear you," he yelled.

Guiltily, she resumed her spaced calls, increasing to one every second or two. After another minute, she heard the sound of crunching leaves close by.

"Here," she called.

"I see you," he said in normal tones.

"Normal" between them meaning he was furious. She stood and tried to pull the thorn off her leg.

"What the hell is so funny?" he demanded, stopping beside her and yanking her free of the vine.

"Your being mad at me," she explained with a giggle. She realized she was on shaky emotional ground.

His grip would have hurt except for the thick padding of her down jacket as he turned her to face him.

"Thank you for coming," she said before he could scold her. She laid her hands on his chest and tried a smile. "I thought...I really thought I was a goner."

Stretching up, she found his chin with her lips, then stepped closer, until she could reach his mouth.

He went very still.

Her relief and gratitude wasn't appeased. She touched his mouth again, needing more from him. Then she ran her tongue along the angry line of his lips. They softened a tiny bit. She needed him desperately.

His grip relaxed. "Damn," he muttered.

His arms slid around her and hauled her against him. She felt his strength enclose her like a blessing. "I was so scared," she whispered, at last able to admit it.

"You scared the devil out of me, too," he said and held her closer. He muttered something, then kissed her.

She held her face up to his kiss and returned it with the same punishing need. Fire shot through her, starting at her lips and plunging all the way to her feet.

She forgot the cold and the snow, the danger of being lost, the helplessness of being blind. Fervently she pushed her hands under his jacket until she could experience his body heat, even through the fleecy mittens.

The hot seeking kisses went on and on...until he pulled away abruptly. "I must be as crazy as you." He took her arm. "Come on. We need to get back before dark."

With terse directions, he guided her through the trees and brush. "I can't believe I came so far," she said.

He snorted. "What were you doing out?"

"I thought I could walk around the backyard without any problem." She paused. "I thought I would know when I got to the trees, that when I touched one I could turn back."

"No one ever walks in a straight line."

"That's why I wasn't worried. I figured I'd go around and come back to the house. Or at least to the road."

Another under-the-breath curse followed this bit of logic. He picked up their pace. The snow was thick now, muffling sound. If he hadn't found her when he did...

"I'm sorry," she said again, feeling worse with every step. "It was a stupid thing to do."

"If you weren't so damn stubborn and determined not to ask anything of anyone, you would have waited until someone could watch you before you ventured into the unknown."

"I've played in these woods all my life."

"Not during the past ten years," he corrected. "Things change. Trees grow. Rocks shift."

"You're right. I was thoughtless and stubborn and really, really stupid—"

"Oh, for Pete's sake," he muttered. "Just shut up."

As they walked, she tried to regain her equilibrium, but like the ground they trod, her emotional landscape was filled with pitfalls she couldn't see. She swallowed painfully and did as she was told.

"We're home," he announced. "Step up."

She touched the concrete slab with her toe and stepped up. They went into the house. The clock chimed, then struck five. Shocked, she realized she'd been in the woods for almost three hours.

"That's the worst thing," she said, thinking aloud as she stuffed the mittens into a pocket and hung up her coat on the coatrack beside the door. "I don't have a sense of time anymore. It's very disorienting."

"Yes, I guess it would be."

His voice was softer, more forgiving, she thought. Then she felt him very close. His sleeve brushed hers. The next thing she knew she was again wrapped against that powerful masculine force again.

The second thing she realized was the strength of his passion. She felt the rock-hard evidence of his hunger against her abdomen. An electrical current scattered in all directions through her body, sending any thoughts she might have had into oblivion.

She clung to him shamelessly, the need hot and urgent in her, too. Running her hands into his hair, still cold from the outdoors, she urged him closer, the kiss harder.

With a low groan, he complied. Lifting her, he swung them both around until the kitchen counter pressed into her hips. She leaned back and opened her mouth to his seeking.

Liquid heat poured through her, carrying her away on a tide of hunger she'd never before experienced, except with him.

"Need you," she whispered in wanton desperation. "Want you."

"How far? How much?" he demanded.

She kissed the side of his face, down his neck until she reached his shirt collar. "I don't know. I don't have answers."

"Neither do I. Only questions. And they suddenly don't matter a damn."

The words slid helplessly from her mind when his fingers slipped between them. She felt them at her shirt buttons. She reached for his, following his example.

Then there was sheer ecstasy as skin touched skin. She heard him gasp as they touched, her hands going around him to caress his back, his doing the same to her.

For the first time, she understood something about the sharing of passion...that it was a mutual thing...the need and the pleasure equally mixed.

His hands moved to her shoulders, pushing her shirt out of the way. She shrugged and felt it fall down her arms and to the floor. When his mouth touched her sensitive skin just above her bra, she felt faint. With a gentle tug, he pulled the satin aside. Then his mouth continued its foray, leaving a sizzling trail in its wake as he explored her more fully. Sensation poured over her in unceasing waves.

"Ohh," she said, breathless.

"Yeah," he agreed, nuzzling the tip of her breast into a pebbled bead of need. "It's strong. Unlike anything I've ever experienced."

"Yes, but why?" she managed to say in spite of the fire running wild in her.

He lifted her to the counter and hollowed out a space for himself between her thighs. "Because..." he said, taking a ragged breath as he pressed ever closer. "Give me your mouth. I need it after the scare you gave me."

"Dangerous," she whispered, "so dangerous."

"Yes. But good. So damn good."

He caressed her in relentless strokes of pure sensation, his broad palms cupping her breasts, his thumbs moving lightly over the nipples, which were growing so sensitive she could feel their constricted outline against the material of her bra. "Take it off."

His deft fingers made quick work of the task. Then she felt an even more wonderful sensation as his chest brushed hers, tormenting her with a thousand delights.

"Rory…"

"Don't talk. Not now."

He sounded desperate. His lips explored her ear, her neck, then along her collarbone. She held her breath until he touched her breast then found the nipple and drew it gently into his mouth, then she sighed.

With hands that trembled, she stroked his back, his sides, then his chest. "It's more than I expected," she admitted, pressing hungry kisses into his hair and on his temple. "This passion. This hunger."

She slid closer and rubbed against him, drawing a low groan from him as she experimented with this new craving that shot through her in bursts of overwhelming pleasure.

He rubbed against her in the most mind-destroying way until she was wild with need too great to be ignored.

"Please," she whispered as his lips touched hers again. "Please. I ache. Everywhere."

"So do I, darlin'. So do I."

His intensity, the demanding male passion, thrilled her. He cupped her breasts, then went still. "Either we finish this, or we stop," he said, his tone warning that they had moved beyond mere kisses. "Which is it to be?"

She laid her head against his chest and heard the thunder of his heart, beating in time to hers. "I want everything." She could hardly speak.

"Be sure."

She didn't want to think. She wanted him to move against her, to bathe her with sensation so thought wasn't necessary. But she knew that wasn't fair. She was a partner in this strange wild passion they shared.

She touched his face with both hands, holding it between them the way he gently held her breasts. She stared blindly up at him, her entire being focused on them, caught up in the magic. She envisioned his face, his eyes.

Then, for a second, she was aware of the sky.

She shook her head slightly. No, not of the sky, but of a shade of blue the color of the sky on a cloud-less day, so brilliant it almost hurt to gaze into its bright hue.

"Do we proceed?" he asked in a low, rasping tone. "Or do we regain our sanity and quit now?"

She put her hands over her face, pressing her palms over her eyes, confused by all the strange questions running through her along with the still-burning passion.

"I think," she began, "I think we have to stop."

His hands fell away from her. She felt the distance as an acute loss. It added its own pain to the turmoil in her. Tears burned her eyes, swelled in her throat.

"I'm sorry," she whispered, not sure what all the emotion meant.

His sigh was soft, almost tender. "Don't be. There'll be other days."

He touched her chin and lifted her face. She sensed his quick study and longed to kiss him again.

"Take care of yourself," he said in a hoarse voice. "You have bruises on your forehead. Better ice it down."

His footsteps receded from her. She crossed her arms over her bare chest and waited.

The door opened. "Next time...we won't stop then," he told her and left quietly, a promise, low and vibrant, in the words.

She swallowed against the knot of tears and touched her eyelids with her fingertips. She remembered when she'd seen that intense blue. It was when the angel had lifted her in his cool, soothing arms and breathed life back into her body. She'd given up, but he had saved her. When she'd opened her eyes, she'd seen a brilliant light, then the color, pinpointed against the blackness.

His eyes. It must have been his eyes.

Trembling, she found her shirt and pulled it on as a chill rushed over her, leaving her shaken and profoundly disturbed by the episode between them. It had been as frightening as being lost in the woods.

Chapter Eight

A loud hammering forced Shannon out of bed the next morning. She slipped on thick socks before flying down the hall to the kitchen, a thousand questions running through her mind as a male voice called out something in the yard and another answered.

She noticed the sun was up as she yanked open the door. The storm must have moved on during the night. "What's going on?" she called out irritably, positive it had something to do with Rory and that she probably wasn't going to like it.

Cold air rushed over her, and her feet immediately protested the chill of the concrete slab as she stepped outside with a frown.

"Hi, Shannon. It's me. Richie."

She relaxed upon hearing the voice. Richie was the son of a deputy sheriff. She brushed her hair into a semblance of order with her fingers. "What's happening—"

"Good morning," a deeper voice said close by.

"The obnoxious neighbor," she said, fighting for a lightness she was far from feeling. She had spent the night torn by her need to go to him and an equal need to protect herself from foolish hopes.

"Hey, watch it. Guys have feelings, you know," he reprimanded, but with an odd mix of undercurrents in his voice.

"What are you two doing?"

"Actually, there's four of us—me, Richie, Jess and Kyle Herriot. Gene will be over later with a couple of men."

Puzzled, she asked, "Why?"

"To finish the bridge over the creek. I put in the supports earlier in the week. We'll run a line from your back door to mine. Gene's bringing a posthole digger. We're going to put up a rail fence around your backyard." He chuckled. "Then you can roam without getting lost."

She intensely regretted yesterday's stupidity. "That really isn't necessary. I won't get lost again."

"Don't go all stiff-necked on us," he said softly. "It's something the guys can do...to make up for that jerk at the store. You've helped a lot of people, now let them do something for you. Be gracious."

She didn't know whether to be furious or, as he suggested, gracious. Her pride wanted to order them off the place. Her innate courtesy sided with Rory. She'd brought this on herself.

"How about fixing lunch?" he asked.

Surely she hadn't slept the whole morning away. "What time is it?"

"A little past eight. Kate is coming over when she picks up her little girl from nursery school. We should be ready for lunch by then. And, uh, you might get dressed. Not that the pink flannel pajamas aren't fetching, but it makes me think of other things. Night. Bed. Sleeping. That sort of thing."

His voice dropped lower on each word, etching chills along her arms and neck, drawing explicit pictures in her mind that caused the hot ache to start in her abdomen.

She fled into the house.

After dressing and securing her hair neatly in a broad clasp at the back of her neck, she remembered her sunglasses. Picking them up, she stood in front of the bathroom mirror for a minute, recalling those first waking moments. There had been something...

She blinked and stared intently toward the mirror. Nothing. Not a flicker. No starbursts of light. Sighing, she put the glasses on, made up the bed and headed for the kitchen, first to eat breakfast, then to put on something for lunch.

A beef stew would make a hearty meal for men working in the cold, she decided a few minutes later. She mixed the ingredients together in a deep roasting pan and put them in the oven, using her mother's recipe.

There was a cherry pie in the freezer, probably in the last stage of serious freezer burn, but she didn't bake from scratch the way Kate did. She got another idea.

After pulling on her down jacket and mittens, she grabbed her purse and went outside. "Richie?"

"Over here," he called.

She turned in that direction and was momentarily blinded by a streak of light. She put a hand to her temple as a wave of dizziness washed over her, then was gone.

"Yeah?" the teenager said, this time directly in front of her.

"Do you have your driver's license yet?" she asked, recovering from the odd sensation.

"No, but I got my learner's permit last month."

"Great. How about driving me into town? I need to run a couple of errands."

"Sure! Uh, I'd better ask my dad," he amended. "Hey, Dad, is it okay if I drive Shannon to town? She has to run some errands."

"Okay, but no speeding," his father replied, the words stern, but humor in the tone.

"Not a mile over eighty," Richie promised, then laughed. "You ready?" he asked her.

"Yes." She held out the car keys. "You'll have to guide me, I'm afraid."

"No problem," he said easily, taking the keys, then her arm. "Don't forget to step down," he warned.

In town, he cheerfully helped her buy doughnuts and apple fritters at the bakery.

"Boy, those cinnamon buns smell good," he said.

"A dozen cinnamon buns," she said to Melissa, another friend who now helped her parents in the shop.

At the grocery, people kept coming up to her, giving her hugs and asking how she was doing. "Fine," she said. "Just fine." She found she could identify everyone by voice. For some reason, that made her feel more confident.

She directed Richie in selecting milk, coffee, tea, bread and crackers. "Hamburger," she added. "Around two pounds. I'll make chili one night. We'd better get more canned tomatoes, also kidney beans."

"Right."

At the checkout counter, she paid with a credit card. "Guide my hand to the line and I'll scrawl my name," she joked with the cashier, a retired English teacher who had insisted that Shannon convert her careless writing into legible essays.

"If I see any scrawl, you'll stand in the corner for fifteen minutes," the woman threatened.

Laughing, Shannon carried a bag and held her escort's arm as they returned to the car. "It's nice to remember that people care about you," she said.

"Yeah."

"How much snow did we get?" she asked, changing to a neutral subject.

"Less than an inch. The real storm isn't due until tonight or tomorrow."

"So yesterday was just a teaser before the real thing," she said, thinking of her foolish walk and feeling guilty that Rory had thought her so irresponsible that he'd called in help to build a safe pen for her to romp in.

If he hadn't found her, if he'd had to call in the rescue team, she would never have lived it down. Her family would probably lock her up. And rightly so. She had no right to put others in danger from her foolishness. From now on, she would be very careful.

However, she wasn't going to be treated as an invalid, either. She sighed. Life was getting complicated. And she had blamed that all-consuming passion on the adrenaline blast from being lost, but it didn't explain what she'd felt upon hearing his voice this morning. Her blood still hummed noisily from the encounter.

At the house, Richie helped her inside, then loped off, ready to resume work. Gene, the sheriff, greeted her heartily. So did two deputies she recognized by voice. They told her the fence was almost done. She could hear the muted roar of a tractor engine and the constant noise of hammers being applied to nails.

After putting the groceries away, she made a pot of coffee and laid the pastries on plates. "Coffee," she called out the door, yelling to make herself heard over the racket.

"Great. Be there in two shakes," Rory called out.

The men trooped in a few minutes later. They lavishly praised her thoughtfulness as they ate and warmed up. She leaned against the counter and sipped fresh coffee, content for the moment.

"What's cooking?" Rory asked, stopping beside her.

"Stew," she told him. "Lunch at twelve," she said, including the rest of the group.

After the men returned to work, she sliced and buttered French bread, managing to nick her thumb only once. Putting the slices on a baking sheet, she placed it next to the oven. Stabbing the stew with a fork and finding it done, she set it on top of the stove and slid the cherry pie into the hot oven. Kate and Mandy arrived shortly before noon.

"Guess what, Shannon?" Mandy demanded in her bubbling manner as soon as she was inside.

"What?"

"I got a star on all my homework. See?"

Shannon felt papers being thrust into her hands.

"Mandy, Shannon can't see right now, remember?" Kate reminded the child gently.

"It's okay," Shannon said. She took a seat at the table and laid the papers on it. "Here, climb up in my lap and tell me about each one. I want to know all about how great my favorite cousin is doing."

"Hey, I'm your favorite cousin," Kate protested.

The door opened and closed. "No, I am," insisted Megan, bringing a wave of cold air with her into the warm kitchen. "Umm, what smells so good?"

"Beef stew," Shannon told her.

"And pie," Kate added. "I'll put the bread in, then set the table. We'd better use the table leaves."

While the two cousins finished the luncheon preparations, Mandy and Shannon moved aside and went over her papers. Shannon loved the smell of baby shampoo and talc as she held the child on her lap and asked about her drawing and coloring efforts. After that, Mandy sang the ABC song.

"And I can say all the ABCs on my flash cards, too," she concluded proudly.

Shannon gave her a hug. "I knew you were smart the first time I met you."

Kate gathered up the homework. "I was very lucky when Cousin Shannon brought you to my house."

"You thoughted you didn't want a little girl, didn't you?" Mandy said earnestly to her new mom.

"Yes, but I didn't know how special you were until I met you," Kate said.

"To know her is to love her," Shannon said, tickling the four-year-old and laughing when she did. She was aware of the door opening and others entering.

Glancing over her shoulder, she saw a sudden flash of light at the corner of her eye. Puzzled, she stared in that direction, but it didn't happen again.

"Come on, Mandy, it's time to wash up," Jess told his daughter. He scooped her off Shannon's lap.

All of them gathered around the table.

"Scoot up," Rory told her.

He pushed her closer to the table, then took the chair beside her, so close his knee occasionally brushed hers. Kate was to her left. Shannon listened to the conversation without taking part. The men were hurrying because of the coming storm.

"Looks bad," one of the deputies mentioned.

"The clouds are really heavy. It'll be snowing before dark."

"The bridge is finished," Rory told her. "There're two posts beside the porch. Hold the cable on the one to the left and it'll take you to the garage and shed. Grab the cable attached to the right post and it'll guide you to the bridge and then to my back door."

"We have the fence up except for four sections on the far side," Jess took up the report. "We'll get those up before we quit."

"Don't stay out in the storm," she said, worrying about snow and wind chill and all the factors that could cause a person to go into hypothermia without realizing it. "I assure you, I'm not venturing outside in this weather. I've learned my lesson."

"What lesson?" Kate asked.

Shannon realized her cousin didn't know about yesterday's little adventure. Not sure what to say, she glanced toward her right where Rory sat.

"She got restless and took a walk in the woods," he said casually. He chuckled and ruffled her bangs. "Luckily she heard me yelling for her."

"You went outside alone?" This from Megan.

Shannon nodded guiltily. "Yes. It was stupid. When Rory didn't find me in the house, he came searching. I...he saved my life. Again."

"Hardly," he corrected on a humorous note. "Actually I came over hoping she'd invite me to stay for dinner. Her cooking is better than mine."

"Daddy cooked French fries and burned them," Mandy announced indignantly.

That brought a protest from her father and laughter from the others. After sharing the pie, the men filed back outside. The three women worked together to clean up. Mandy helped by putting the silverware in the dishwasher.

"That was fun," Megan said in a quiet tone. "It's nice to have family and friends, isn't it?"

"Yes," Shannon agreed.

"Mandy and I have to run. She's starting piano lessons today, and we don't want to be late for the first one."

Kate and Mandy kissed Shannon goodbye.

"How's Grandfather?" Shannon asked when she and Megan were alone.

"Not so good. He's losing weight and his blood pressure is up again."

"I hope he doesn't have another stroke. Remember how, as children, we were terrified of making him angry?"

"Yes. He had a temper, but he never used it on us kids. I don't know what we found so scary."

They chatted about the past, then Megan left to get ready for the afternoon riding classes. Shannon put on her jacket and mittens and went outside. She found the two posts beside the porch. Taking hold of the left cable, she walked to the shed and garage. Kate and Jess had stored her car there for her. Pleased, she retraced her steps and found the cable from the other post.

Following the new trail, she heard the crunch of gravel under her feet. At the end of the gravel path she discovered a wooden bridge arching over the creek, complete with railings on either side. With a hand on the top rail, she walked over the narrow crossing and found the cable again and the continuation of the gravel.

She hesitated, knowing she was no longer on Windraven land. The path led straight to *his* door.

Retreating to the high point of the little bridge, she stood there breathing in the cold mountain air, sensing the coming storm in the faint scent of ozone that wafted around her. Then she felt a familiar warmth on her face.

The sun had come from behind the clouds, she deduced.

Recalling the strange sense of light from that morning and the odd little flashes she'd experienced since then, she put a hand up to her sunglasses. Quickly, before thinking further on it, she whipped them off and looked toward the warmth coming from the sky.

For only a second. Then she blinked and closed her eyes against the pain that laced through them, the same type of pain one felt upon leaving a dark theater and entering the sunlight. But in the split second of pain, she'd seen that flash of blue again. She trembled with hope and the fear of reading too much into what could be merely a phenomenon of stray electrical current in the optic nerve.

Shakily she slipped the glasses on and, grabbing the cable, hurried to her own door. Inside she tossed the glasses on the counter, then leaned against it with her hands pressed to her eyes.

The door opened and closed quietly.

She dropped her hands and opened her eyes wide, willing her eyes to see.

"What is it?" Rory asked. "What happened out there on the bridge a moment ago?"

Unsure she wanted to share news of the incident, which she feared could have been a fluke of her imagination, she bridled. "Were you spying on me?"

"I was watching," he said, not at all deterred by the accusation in her tone. "Something happened with your eyes. What?"

She turned her back to him and fumbled until she found her glasses and slid them on. "I don't know. Nothing."

His hands clasped her shoulders and turned her around. "Tell me," he said ruthlessly.

His heat surrounded her. His larger size and strength felt dangerous. She was vulnerable to something about him, to a wildness and need she had only vaguely sensed within herself. She glared at him, seeing only darkness but determined not to let him know how much his nearness distressed her.

"I thought I saw something…a flash of blue," she finally admitted, pressing against the counter, feeling trapped although his hold on her was light. "I've seen it before, but nothing changes. Afterwards, it's all darkness."

The silence pressed around them. She lifted her chin and dared him to feel sorry for her.

"I see."

She could tell nothing from his voice, not pity or sympathy or anything.

His hands slid to her neck. With thumbs under her chin, he tilted her head further back. He removed her glasses. She felt exposed without them. His breath caressed her face as he loomed nearer.

"Look at me," he ordered.

She stared at the point his voice came from and tried not to show either the hope she couldn't quite suppress or the fear that wouldn't quite fade.

He moved and she heard a click. She blinked at the sudden bright spot. A click and the brightness disappeared.

"What did you see?"

"I—I don't know."

"Yes, you do," he insisted. "Tell me."

When she would have pressed her hands over her eyes, he caught both wrists and put them behind her back, holding her there, his chest brushing hers as he bent over her, his silence demanding an answer to his questions, his hold gentle but firm, telling her she couldn't escape.

"Watch," he said softly.

A click, the slight flare of brightness, then another click and it was gone.

"What did you see?"

She took a shaky breath. "A sort of brightness...like a streetlight through fog, very dense fog...but it doesn't last."

"It will," he murmured, his mouth close to hers. "It will," he repeated, fiercely this time as if he defied some unseen foe to deny it.

His mouth came down on hers. She turned her head, needing to get away, to think, to let the whirl of confused emotion inside her settle, to cry…

But not in front of him.

Keeping her hands behind her back with one hand, he used the other to bring her face to his. Then he kissed her, his mouth without pity or tenderness, only wild harsh demand that reached down into her being, to that place of untamed hunger, wild with its own unfulfilled need.

She moved her head from side to side, not in protest but…she didn't know what. As if they were locked in mortal combat, he followed her movement, refusing to release her hands or her mouth.

He made a low, hardly audible sound deep in his throat, and she understood that he struggled with this strange passion between them as greatly as she did. With a sigh, she gave up the battle and arched against him, letting their heat join and surround them with the unique fire they stirred in each other.

Slipping a hand around her shoulders, he bent to her, his body arching over hers, matching curve to curve—thigh and stomach and chest.

Rory knew he should get out of there, that she was vulnerable and he was heartless to take advantage of it, but nothing mattered at the moment but the feel of her body against his, that mind-shattering combination of soft yielding and firm resistance.

Her lips moved against his, not denying but responding, feeding his hunger with hers, no longer struggling against feelings too powerful to ignore. He drank in her sweetness as if it were nectar while a song of wild triumph sang through his blood.

When he could no longer pull enough air into his lungs, he had to release her mouth. Breathing harshly, he rested his head against hers and tried to think of cool things to chill his blood.

"Madness," she said, a muted whisper of confused despair.

It stabbed him straight in the heart. Opening his eyes, he started to speak, then saw Kate's husband watching them through the window, his expression one of dark anger.

"Time to face the music," he murmured, forcing himself to fight the riptide of hunger and longing that had sucked them both into its whirlpool.

"What music?"

He realized she was still lost in the passion. He drew away and studied her face. Her eyes were smoky blue, her expression one of bewilderment. He knew she couldn't see, but he smiled anyway as something new and fragile flooded him. He couldn't recall feeling tenderness for a woman, not deep down, soul-plucking tenderness. It worried him.

"Time for me to get back to work," he told her gently and released her.

She laid her hands on the counter at her sides, found her glasses and slipped them on with hands that trembled slightly. He noted the tremble and realized he wanted to make love to her until they were both sated...

But not now.

"See you later," he said and headed outside.

Kate's husband was waiting. "What's going on?" Jess asked. "Was that a mutual kiss I witnessed or did you force it on her?"

Rory shot the other man a warning glance. "What do you think?" he asked in a snarl. Yeah, how to win friends and influence a woman's relatives, he mocked, but he wasn't ready to talk about it yet.

"I thought she was struggling at first," Jess admitted, "then I decided maybe she wasn't. I didn't want to barge in like an irate father if she started it."

Rory exhaled heavily. "She didn't, but…she didn't exactly say no, either."

Jess was silent for a long moment. He watched Gene and the sheriff fit a rail between two posts at the far end of the yard before he nailed Rory with a sharp gaze.

"She's vulnerable," he said, his tone neutral while he delivered the reminder.

"I'd wait until her sight returned if I was sure it would," Rory replied. "She's seeing…having flashes of light, but she's not sure if it's vision or something else."

"That makes it more important for you to leave her alone. She doesn't need the confusion of sex on top of her other worries."

Rory frowned. "How do you know what she needs?" he demanded, keeping his tone low as the anger rose.

"I don't. Neither do you. You're thinking with something besides your head if you think you do. Give her space and a chance to find her own way. Kate and Megan are worried, too."

Rory muttered an expletive. "Has the whole county voiced an opinion on the subject?" he asked coldly.

Jess grinned. "Probably. You started it with that demonstration in the diner. That was all over town in a matter of hours."

"That damn lawyer." Rory fought a strong impulse to drive to town and strangle the bastard.

"I agree. She certainly didn't need him." Jess leveled a gaze on him again. "Don't make her need you, then walk out when the need becomes too great."

Rory watched the deputy's son nail the last rail in place, then the teenager and the sheriff gathered up the tools, looked at the dark clouds that totally covered the sky and headed across the yard.

"I won't hurt her," he heard himself say.

A promise.

"Okay." Jess walked off and opened the camper on the back of his truck so Richie could store the hammers and crosscut saw they'd brought to the job.

When the men had said farewell, first to Shannon, then to him, they drove off, heading home before the storm hit.

Rory checked their handiwork. The posts were secure, the fence sturdy. He looked at Shannon's house for a long, soul-struggling moment, then walked across the bridge in the falling snow to his own dark, empty home.

Chapter Nine

*K*nock. *Knock.*

Shannon hit the stop button on the portable tape player, halting the audio version of the book she'd been listening to.

The summons came again, at the front door, she realized. She rose from the sofa and made her way to the entrance. There, she hesitated. Only a stranger would come to the front of the house. Friends and family would park at the side and come in through the kitchen.

Realizing she was nervous in dealing with the unknown, she steeled herself and opened the door a few inches, her foot braced behind it to stop its being thrust open before she could react. "Yes?"

"Excuse me, ma'am," a male voice said. "I was wondering…that is, I'm looking for work. I wondered if you had anything you needed done, or if you could recommend a ranch around here that might need help?"

Shannon considered the request. It sounded reasonable. Except no cowboy would apply for ranch work in the dead of winter. All the cattle were in the home pastures. Other than feeding and keeping an eye on the herd, which could be done by one or two men even on the largest spreads, there was nothing much to do until the spring calving started.

"I'm sorry, but I don't know of anyone who needs help now. You might try some of the larger spreads in a couple of months when calving starts." She forced herself to smile. "Good luck."

"Thanks. Sorry to trouble you."

"No problem." She closed the door and clicked the dead bolt on. Standing there, she listened as a motor fired up and receded down the road. A pickup, she decided, with an uneven beat, as if it misfired on one cylinder every little bit.

Nervous and restless for no reason she could discern, she went and locked the back door, too. After that she prowled the house, checking all the windows and making sure they were also locked.

Sitting on the sofa, she didn't resume her book on tape, but sat there lost in thought. As a cop, she knew that when instinct told a person there was something wrong about a stranger, there usually was. Some kind of signal was being sent that said this wasn't quite right.

That's how she felt about the cowboy looking for work. In January? In Wyoming? Drifting cowboys followed a spring-through-fall circuit that started south and worked north. They certainly didn't start in Canada and work their way south through the winter.

So what had he really been after?

There was one person who would be interested in her. The man at the gas station. What if he wanted to find out if she could see? From the newspaper reports, he would know she'd possibly been blinded by his shot, but now he might want to be sure, especially if he was planning further mischief in these parts and wanted to know if she could identify him.

Or was her imagination working overtime?

She laughed at herself, feeling foolish for her fears. After all, didn't she have a watchful neighbor right next door, one who thought it his duty to check on her daily?

Except he hadn't last night. She'd heard his truck arrive home at seven. Since she'd heard him leave at six-thirty that morning, she knew he'd put in a twelve-hour day.

The promised storm had come in Monday night. It had snowed all day Tuesday, dropping over eight inches. The roads would have been dangerous. Between doing his job and dealing with the weather, Rory must have been dead tired by the time he got home. He'd gone out again around seven this morning and hadn't come home for lunch.

Not that she cared. It was merely an observation on her part. Her heart thudded heavily all at once, as if belying her conclusion. The clock chimed the half hour, reminding her of the casserole she'd put in the oven an hour ago.

She turned the oven off and put a lid on the oven-proof bowl so the dinner wouldn't burn. Umm, smelled good. If she'd known the cowboy who came to the door, she would have invited him to stay to eat.

Hearing another vehicle on the road, she listened intently as it drew closer. She recognized it easily.

Glancing toward the window, she wondered if Rory had planned anything for the evening meal. Recalling his tomato soup and grilled cheese sandwiches, she figured he hadn't. She owed him for finding her in the woods and for building the bridge and fence.

After thinking about it for another minute, she slipped on snow boots, jacket and mittens. With the casserole in a basket trivet in one hand, she went outside and felt for the cable. Finding it, she stepped gingerly off the porch into the snow.

It was more of a challenge than she'd thought it would be, balancing the casserole in one hand, holding on with the other and sinking into the ankle-deep snow with every step. Luckily her boots were knee-high.

At the bridge, she relaxed. Halfway there. Then her foot skidded and she plopped down on her behind with a thud and an unlady-like expression.

Frowning, she sat in the snow and took stock.

She'd managed to keep her peace offering from spill-ing; that had been her first concern when her foot slipped. Neither was she hurt. She stood, grabbed the railing and marched on.

After a few steps, she realized the snow had been shoveled on this side of the path. That made walking a lot easier. She hurried to his back door and knocked.

No answer.

Hmm, he might be in the garage doing something. Or in the shower. She could slip in, leave the casse-role and beat a hasty retreat.

Scared? part of her mocked.

Not at all. Well, maybe. Their kisses were so wild and soul-stirring....

Giving an impatient *huh,* she tried the door and found it open. So much for his lecturing her on safety.

She tiptoed into the kitchen and felt along the counter until she came to the stove. She set the bowl down and turned, intending to sneak out and get home before he found her in his house uninvited—

"Smells good," a masculine voice said. "What is it?"

"Oh!" she gasped, a hand going to her pounding heart. "You startled me," she said, an accusation.

He laughed in a low, husky manner that added bursts of electricity to her erratic heartbeats.

"Not as much as you startled me, sneaking into a man's house like a thief," he said. "I was wondering what you were up to when I saw you through the bedroom window."

She'd forgotten about the windows that faced her house. "Did you see—" She stopped.

"The fall? Yes. Rather gracefully done, I must say."

She frowned in his direction. "Is there anything you don't notice?"

His laughter was delicious—as sweet to her senses as a caress, as promising of fulfillment as the love play between them. "Maybe. Fortunately, you can't return the favor."

She tilted her head, trying to figure out the nuances behind the words. "So?"

"I'd just stepped out of the shower when I noticed you on the bridge."

Visions flooded into her mind. "Are you...aren't you...?"

"I'm not," he said, laughter rippling over the words.

Heat flamed into her face. "I'll be going," she said stiffly. "So you can dress and eat before the food gets cold."

"Coward," he murmured. "Stay and eat. You never did tell me what you fixed."

"A Mexican casserole. It's made with hamburger and corn and cornmeal, sort of like chili but..." She edged toward the door. "I really should be getting home. Before it's too dark," she added, then realized how inane that sounded. As if it made any difference to her.

She never made it to the door. His hand on her arm stopped her before she'd taken more than two steps.

"Stay," he said, an order and a request.

Feeling his warmth, she put out her hands to hold him off, knowing she was too susceptible to his kisses. She encountered bare flesh. She gasped and jerked back.

"It's okay," he assured her. "I'm decent."

He took one hand and led it down his torso to his waist. She encountered a waistband. "Sweats?"

"Yes," he said.

She sighed in relief, drawing a laugh from him.

"'Fraidy-cat," he mocked lightly.

Pulling free, she said, "Not at all. I simply believe in self-preservation."

"Have a seat. I'll get a shirt on, then set the table. Milk or beer?"

"Uh, milk."

Before she could think of a reason she had to leave, she found herself in a chair at his table, her coat and mittens off. His footsteps retreated down the hall, then returned in less than a minute. She heard him move around the kitchen, then take his place at the small round table. He dished up the casserole.

"I made us each a salad," he told her. "A glass of milk is to the right of your plate."

"Thanks. Tell me about your kitchen. What does it look like?"

"Old. It's outdated. After seeing what you did at your place, I've decided to replace the cabinets and modernize."

"It's a fun project. You should ask Kate for ideas.

She's really good at decorating. First you have to decide on a color scheme.''

"I like blue."

Shannon wrinkled her nose. "It's men's favorite color, but I think it's too cool for a home. I like warmer colors."

"Passionate," he murmured.

"I beg your pardon?"

A hand briefly touched her hair.

"Your colors are red and gold. Fire and precious metal. But you used a sort of cream and sage green in your house. I thought green was a cool color."

She smoothed the hair at her temple where he'd stroked. "Green is neutral. I chose it because of the sagebrush. I like its toughness and the way it grows even in the most adverse conditions."

"It's tenacious. Like you."

The compliment warmed her like brandy on a cold night, and brought forth a confession. "I'd given up," she said somberly, "when I was shot. It was your touch that called me back from the darkness. The pain was so great, then you were there, so cool and bright, like an angel...." She stopped, embarrassed.

He didn't say anything. The silence felt tremulous and uncertain. She really wished she'd learn to keep her mouth shut about silly things.

"Eat," he finally said in a very soft tone.

Picking up a fork, she did as he suggested. After a couple of minutes, he began speaking of his day, of the operations he performed for the Humane Society twice a month, of the old bull that had died and the old rancher who'd nearly been in tears over it.

"The old names are dying out," he concluded. "Kids don't want the hardship and uncertainty of ranch life."

"And the isolation. It's also easier to make a living in the city," she added.

He nodded and asked, "So why did you give up your place in town?"

"Crazy, wasn't it?" Shannon agreed. "I felt I needed more space, a quiet place to go at the end of the day. I planned to have my practice in town, my home out here."

"Mm, we need to get started on the notes for your degree, don't we?"

"Who's we?" she quipped smartly. "As I recall, it's my job."

"You'll need help. I'll read the notes to you."

"I wouldn't foist my handwriting on anyone, but thanks anyway."

His hand closed over hers. "It isn't going to do you any good to refuse," he advised quite gently.

She started to argue, but just then she heard the sound of an engine. She listened intently.

"What?" Rory asked.

"That truck. It's the same guy who stopped at my place earlier today and asked about a ranching job. In January."

She heard Rory's chair scrape on the floor, then his sock feet hitting the floor at a near run. Cold air stirred around her as a door opened in the front of the house. He returned in another couple of minutes.

"It's a pickup with a camper shell on the back. Black or dark blue, I think. Colorado license plate. He stopped at your place?"

"Yes." She laughed. "I immediately decided he was the perp from the gas station, checking to see if I could identify him." She laughed again so he would know she realized how foolish this notion was.

He didn't join in. "You could be right. I'll mention it to Jess. He can check with the other deputies on any strangers lingering around town."

"Really, that isn't necessary. No need to alarm him or Kate over something that probably means nothing. Please, I'd rather you didn't say anything."

"Okay," he agreed reluctantly. "Do you know my phone number?"

"No."

"Memorize it. Call me if...no. I'll run a line from my house to yours. All you'll have to do is hit a button and I'll come running." This time he did laugh. "Real quick, darling."

She huffed in exasperation. "You'll do no such thing. I know how to dial 911 if I need help."

"I'm closer. If you'll keep making food like this, I'll come over every night and check your place for bogeymen."

"Ha-ha," she said.

The conversation was becoming fraught with innuendo. She was aware of him on her right, of the fact that her foot touched his every once in a while if she wasn't very careful when she moved her feet.

She wiped her mouth and thought of his kisses. When he teased and called her "darling," she couldn't help but respond, even though she knew he didn't mean it as an endearment.

Life with him would be fun. If he loved her. If she loved him. She froze, horrified at the idea.

Rory was ten times more attractive than any man she'd ever met. And a hundred times more dangerous to her heart.

He couldn't help his looks, but, face it, he could have any woman he wanted. Right now there was passion between them, but that didn't mean they would also share a lasting love. Although it would be nice to think so...

Actually his interest in her might be due to the injury and him finding her. Danger forged bonds between people, and he was a naturally protective person.

While she was overwhelmingly drawn to him, a wise woman should guard her heart against such temptations of the flesh. And so she would, she vowed.

"So what do you think?" Rory asked Jess Fargo, chief of investigations for the sheriff's office and cousin to Shannon by virtue of being married to Kate.

"I can't arrest a man for inquiring about a job or being out on a public road," Jess answered, but his eyes reflected worry. "Hold on a minute."

Rory waited while Jess went to a file cabinet and returned with a folder. Inside were pictures of the crime scene that Rory had witnessed—the three bodies on the floor with blood everywhere.

"Look at this," Jess said. "Recognize him?"

"It was the other man at the gas station."

"If you see him around Shannon's place, let me know."

Rory handed the picture back. "And that's it? That's all you can do?"

Jess nodded. "Shannon thinks there wasn't another man, but the gun had disappeared. There just isn't any evidence unless she or the owner can identify the other guy as the robber."

"The man could have stayed conscious long enough to hide the gun. Did you look in the trash cans?"

Jess gave him a pained look.

"Okay, okay, just asking," Rory said. He stood. "I've got to get back for afternoon office hours. After that, I'm going home and sleeping for twelve hours. Anybody who wakes me will be in big trouble."

"I hear you," Jess said sympathetically. "We had a break-in at the diner around midnight. Couple of teenagers reported it. If they'd been at home instead of out cruising at that hour, no one would have noticed the door jimmied open, and I'd have gotten a full night's sleep."

Rory chuckled, then left the lawman and went to his office. He got through his afternoon appointments without getting bitten, kicked or chewed out by a patient's owner. That meant it was a good day.

He was on the road home shortly after five. New clouds were forming over the western peaks, but he could tell the days were growing longer by the lingering traces of light in the sky. Soon it would be spring again.

The lambing season would begin. Calves would arrive. Chicks would hatch. New life would be bursting out everywhere in the trees and hills, the lakes and streams.

Everywhere but his place. He shrugged off the emptiness induced by the thought of his house. He would marry soon and fill it with kids. As soon as he found the woman.

The librarian or the schoolteacher?

A low ache pounded through his body in time to the thud of his heart. He had to get Shannon out of his mind first.

Shannon tied one end of a ball of string to a nail she'd pounded into the frame by the front door. She carried the ball with her as she headed for the mailbox. Rory or Kate or Megan had brought in her mail the prior three days. It was time she did it herself.

She reached the road without mishap, but found the mailbox on its side, still attached to the wooden post, which was knocked out of the ground. Vandals, she supposed, or someone who took the curve too fast and skidded off the road a bit.

Holding the string in her teeth, she propped the post

in its hole and tamped the soggy ground around it. When she let go, the mailbox leaned to the side at a forty-degree angle. She needed a shovel.

After placing the ball of string in the mailbox, she went back to the house and out the back door. Holding the cable, she made it to the shed and found the tool. She brought the hoe, too. It might come in handy.

She retraced her path to the road, then laid the mailbox and post aside in order to dig the muck out of the hole. She removed her gloves and gathered some rocks to drop into the bottom, then repositioned the post and shoveled dirt in, tamping it down with the hoe every inch or so.

Her heart kicked up when she heard a vehicle on the road coming from town, but slowed when she realized it wasn't Rory. She paused and listened. She recognized the truck with the missing beat.

The stranger stopped.

She heard him get out and slam the door. "Hello," she called, gripping the hoe tightly with both hands.

"Hey there," he said. "I'm sort of lost and wondered if you could help me."

She nodded, her suspicion increasing at his too-friendly tone and the fact that he didn't mention he'd been out there looking for a job just two days ago.

"I was looking for Mulholland Creek Road. A friend, Bob Robertson, lives on it, but I can't find his place."

"Robertson," she repeated as if mulling it over.

"You have the right road, but there's no one by that name on it that I know of. Sorry."

"Well, thanks anyway."

She waited for him to leave, but he didn't.

"Say, looks like you could use some help there."

"I can manage," she said quickly.

"I'll just take the shovel and add a little dirt to one side. I think that'll take care of it. There's a couple of good-size rocks over there, too. I'll put them on each side to add some weight."

"That's all right," she told him, but he didn't take the hint.

He shoveled some dirt around the post, then used the hoe to tamp it in. "Can you grab those couple of smaller rocks there and I'll get the big ones?"

"Where? I can't see."

"Oh," he said, as if surprised. "Oh, I'm sorry, ma'am. I didn't realize...but that's what the dark glasses are for, aren't they? I'm really sorry."

"It's okay. Really."

"Well, here, I'll just finish this." He handed the tools back to her. She heard him stacking the rocks.

"There," he said. "I put some rocks around the post to make it more stable. That should hold now. Is there anything else I can do?"

She plucked the ball of string out of the mailbox. "Would you tie an end around the post, then cut it?"

"Sure. There you are, all done." He pressed the string into her hand.

"Thanks for your help. I hope you find your friend," she said. She lifted the shovel and hoe and, grabbing the string, walked back to the house. Once inside, she flicked the dead bolt and stood there until she heard the truck leave, its engine pinging until it faded into silence.

After placing the tools on the back porch, she locked that door, too, and removed a TV dinner from the oven. She remembered to turn on the light before she sat down to eat the lonely meal.

She caught herself concentrating on the house next door. At last she heard Rory's truck on the road. It turned into his driveway, paused—while the garage door opened, she assumed—then pulled into the garage and shut off. She wondered if he would come over.

If he did, he wouldn't find supper waiting. It would be a cold day you-know-where before she would treat him to another meal. She didn't need the hassle of dealing with him and his libido...or her own, she admitted.

The ring of the telephone startled her into a gasp. She quickly picked up the kitchen unit. "Hello?"

"Hi, it's me. You ready for dinner?"

"I've just finished," she informed him coolly.

There was a brief silence. "Okay, you can have dessert while I eat. How about the steak house down on the interstate?"

"That's an hour's drive."

"Uh-huh," he agreed. "It'll take me fifteen minutes to shower and change. Casual dress. Will you need more time?"

She started to refuse, then thought of the stranger.

Coward, she called herself, taking the easy way out. "Yes, I'll be ready. Shall I come over there?"

"Sure. The back door will be open."

Laughter spun through his voice like golden threads wrapping around her heart. He hung up. She did so more slowly, the allure of him, of spending the evening with him, running through her like honey.

She touched the scar at her temple. Foolish, oh, so foolish, but she was going.

Dashing into her bedroom, she changed to black wool slacks with a matching jacket and a black and gold knit turtleneck. She found her dress boots and dusted them off. With a small black purse that attached at her waist, she was ready. She combed her hair, but left it loose, then put on lipstick, afraid to try anything more elaborate in makeup.

Grabbing warm mittens, she draped her down coat around her shoulders, then walked over to Rory's house.

The snow had been removed from her side of the path, too. When did he find time to do all that?

"Hi, I'm here," she said upon entering the kitchen.

"Be with you in a sec," he called out.

From his bedroom, she guessed. The house had once belonged to Kate's mother-in-law, and Shannon had been in it a couple of times long ago. It had three or four bedrooms, a big kitchen plus a dining room, living room and a parlor.

There was a huge pantry off the kitchen, if she remembered right. A second bathroom had been added to the largest bedroom at one time, making it into a master suite.

A family house, meant for husband, wife and kids.

She wondered what woman would get to help him redecorate it, then winced as a painful contraction shot through her. It was none of her business.

Remember that and you won't get hurt, she reminded her softer, sentimental side. She wasn't going to be that woman. She wasn't going to fall in love with Rory Daniels and be left with a hole in her heart when he got over feeling sorry for her, or whatever, and went off to new pastures. She was too wise for that.

Really. She was. Definitely.

Chapter Ten

"Is it snowing?" Shannon asked. "I forgot to catch the news tonight."

"No, the sky is clear, and you can see a million stars," Rory said. "The moon is riding high over Medicine Bow Peak, like a big silver dollar hanging in the sky. It isn't quite full yet, but it's getting there."

"Sounds lovely."

There was a half beat of silence, then, "Yeah, lovely," he said huskily.

A frisson started somewhere in the middle of her belly and zipped through every nerve. She knew he meant her. She clutched her hands together in her lap and didn't respond.

"The snow is thick on the trees," he continued, "making the world a fairyland. The firs are graceful ladies all decked out for a ball."

She smiled as she pictured the scene.

"We're on the ramp to the interstate. Now we're merging into the right lane. Traffic is light and the road is clear. The snowplows were out all last night and today."

He kept up a running commentary all the way to the steak house. Shannon relaxed and enjoyed the descriptive monologue. At the restaurant, he told her to wait, then came around and opened the door. With her hand tucked into the curve of his arm, they went inside.

Music blasted her ears, drowning out all other sound. She flinched, suddenly nervous at the noise. Rory covered her hand with his.

"It's okay," he said. "Nothing to worry about."

He took her coat and mittens. When she was seated in a booth, he excused himself and left. She swallowed against the fear that suddenly clogged her throat. He wasn't abandoning her, for goodness sake.

But she listened intently for any ominous sounds as she sipped a cool drink of water and tried to act normally. The music became quieter all at once. She could now detect the presence of other people at surrounding tables—the clink of cutlery against plates, voices, the passage of a couple being led to their table behind her.

Rory returned and slid in beside her. "Ah, that's much better."

"Did you ask them to turn the music down?"

"Yes. It was so loud a person couldn't think."

Warmth crept through her. "Thank you."

A hand touched her hair, caressed her shoulder. "Anything for my lady," he said in that husky tone he'd used before, the one that promised the world and the moon and the stars, all for her.

"Wine?" he asked.

"Yes, red, please."

He ordered a merlot for each of them, then the house steak specialty for himself. "Umm, delicious," he told her when the food arrived. "You like steak?"

"Yes."

"Open up."

"That's okay—"

A morsel of meat was expertly placed in her mouth. She chewed and swallowed. "I have to admit, that's better than the TV dinner I had earlier."

He chuckled. "How do you like your baked potato, with everything?"

"Yes. Lots of sour cream."

"You got it."

"But really—"

"Yes, really," he murmured before she could protest. "I like sharing with you."

His presence was like a force field along her right side. She slid into the corner of the booth, separating them as much as possible. "This isn't a good thing."

"I beg to differ. It's very good. Open up."

She gave up arguing, and he continued to feed her as he ate. The act was so intimate, his voice so sexy, his attention so focused, she felt they were nearly making love right there in public. Inside, she went all warm and shaky and apprehensive.

He ordered the mud pie for dessert. She recalled that it was huge, enough for three or four people.

"Open," he murmured.

She did.

He placed a spoonful of cool ice cream and warm chocolate sauce on her tongue. She felt a drip on her chin. Before she could wipe it off, he did it for her.

"You should go into child care," she quipped, trying to dispel the sensuous mood. "You'd be good at it."

"I plan to. I want kids, don't you?"

She blinked, stunned by the announcement, then she thought of him surrounded by children, playing with them, teaching them to care for their pets, of them helping him tend injured wildlife.

"Don't you?" he asked again, more insistent this time.

"I—I plan to work with children and their families when I get my license."

"But what about a family of your own?"

"Do you think that will happen?" she demanded, the anger breaking through as pain shredded her heart. "Who would want a..." she forced herself to say it "...a blind person?"

He moved close, his thigh against hers, hemming her into the corner. "Me. I want you."

She tried to breathe evenly. It was impossible. She

managed a disdainful laugh. "Yes, but we've already established that you're weird."

"Crazy," he corrected softly. "As in—crazy for you."

He laughed and moved back, giving her space to breathe again. She took a ragged breath. "Are you finished? I'm tired. I'd like to go home."

He called for the check. On the ride home, she stayed close to the door on her side of the bench seat. Another person could easily have sat in the space between them.

When he stopped, she heard the sound of a garage door going up. They were at his house. She tensed. He led her into the house through the room she remembered was a pantry and into the kitchen.

"I'll make some coffee," he said.

"None for me. I'm going home."

He was in her face in an instant, his hands on her upper arms. "Stay."

The word was a demand, but it wasn't harsh. Beneath it ran an undercurrent, almost like a plea. Tremors rushed through her. She felt caught in a torrent of desire and painful need that was more than passion.

"I can't," she whispered. "Please. I can't."

He caressed her shoulders, rubbing soothing circles with his thumbs. "You're frightened. Why?"

She pressed her lips together and shook her head. "It's too confusing to explain."

Silence pulsated between them. She waited, expecting his lips to descend on hers at any second. But at last he sighed and stepped back. "I'll walk you home."

"That isn't necessary."

"Yeah, it is, lady cop."

She let him escort her from his door to hers. He saw her safely inside, told her to lock the door and left.

Alone, she leaned against the counter and wrapped her arms across her chest, feeling spent and yet restless. With the perversity of human nature, she now wished she'd stayed with him.

All night?

Yes. Yes!

She closed her eyes in despair. She was afraid she was very close to doing the one thing she'd vowed not to do—fall in love with her handsome neighbor.

Shannon opened her eyes and stared into the darkness. What had jarred her out of a sound sleep?

She listened intently. The hair stood up on the back of her neck. She knew that sound. It was the truck with the uneven beat, the one belonging to the stranger who had stopped by twice that week. She hardly dared breathe as she heard it cruise past her house, going very slowly.

Then it stopped.

Clutching the comforter to her breast, she waited to hear the truck move on toward town. But there was no sound at all. He'd killed the engine.

Less than a tenth of a mile down the road was a pull-off and a snow shelter for kids who had to wait for the school bus. It sounded as if he'd stopped there. Why?

To come back and break into her house?

A blind woman alone would be easy prey, whether the intent was robbery...or worse.

The clock in the living room played its preliminary melody, then struck the hour. One o'clock.

Without waiting another second, she slid out of bed. Grabbing her dark blue robe—a good camouflage color for going out into the night—she slipped it on while gliding soundlessly down the hall. In the kitchen, she pulled on her insulated boots, then eased out the back door.

Fear clawed at her neck as she sped down the snowy path. At any moment she expected to be grabbed from behind and forced back into the house. Knees stiff, she crossed the icy bridge without a sound, then raced to Rory's door.

She found it unlocked. As soon as she was inside, she clicked the dead bolt into place, then fled along the hall, her hands touching each wall until she came to a doorway. She went inside the room.

"Rory?" she said softly, as if the stranger might hear and barge in and shoot them on the spot.

"What? Shannon? What is it?"

"Someone stopped on the road, down by the snow shelter, I think. It...it frightened me."

A flash of light made her blink. She realized she'd forgotten her glasses. As if that mattered.

Rory threw the covers off, paused, then shrugged. It wasn't as if he were flaunting himself in front of

Shannon. Although she stood in his bedroom, her eyes wide and dark with apprehension, he knew she couldn't see the reaction of his body to her presence at...five after one in the morning, he noted on the digital clock.

Realizing his bedside light could be seen from her bedroom, he clicked off the lamp and grabbed the dark gray sweats he'd left on the floor. "I'll check it out," he told Shannon, throwing on the clothing and some socks.

"No, don't go out. He has a gun."

"How do you know?"

She shook her head. "I know he's the robber who shot me. I can't prove it, but I know it. He's armed and dangerous. Call the sheriff's office—wait!"

"What?"

She held up a hand, turning her head slightly to catch the sound. "He's leaving. He's heading for town."

"Okay. I'll let the sheriff know."

Rory picked up the phone by the bed and dialed the dispatcher. He reported someone had stopped by Shannon's house and was now on the road back to town. No, he didn't want the guy picked up—he hadn't done anything—but Rory wanted a license plate number, if possible, for Jess to check out. He hung up and turned on the light again.

Shannon stared toward the light, her hands in the pockets of the blue robe, a worried frown on her face. The collar of her pink pajamas was visible at the neck of the robe. She looked enticingly disheveled. His body went rigid.

Nothing unusual in that. It happened at the mere thought of her, not to mention what actually seeing her did, especially at this hour and in her nightclothes.

"Come on. We could use that coffee. I'll make some decaf. I even have pastries I was planning to bring over to your place in the morning. Thoughtful, huh?"

"Yes."

She sounded uncertain, causing him to smile. Yeah, he knew what it was to be unsure around a person of the opposite sex, although it wasn't something he'd experienced in a long while.

In the kitchen, he put on the coffee, then placed chocolate eclairs on two plates and warmed them for a few seconds in the microwave. "Here we go," he said with fake cheer as he placed them on the table.

He poured the coffee when the maker stopped gurgling and joined his guest at the table. Neither of them was hungry, although he had to give her credit for trying a couple of bites, then she laid the pastry on the plate, pushed it aside and leaned her forehead against her hands.

"I hate this, hate this, hate this," she said.

He swallowed the bite that seemed to grow bigger as he chewed. He wanted to comfort her, but wasn't sure that was what she needed. Or if he could stop at that.

"It's tough," he agreed.

"Sometimes I think it's over, that I'm going to be

able to see...like the light in your room when you turned it on. It *seemed* as if I could see it, but then everything goes dark again.''

Rory couldn't stand the despair in the slump of her shoulders. He went to her. "I know, darling," he murmured and lifted her into his arms.

She turned her face to him, a question in her beautiful eyes. He wondered how, without sight, she seemed able to peer into his soul.

"You'll spend the rest of the night here," he told her, preparing for an argument.

After a tense second, she nodded.

He carried her to his room. "This is the only bed in the house. Don't worry. You'll be safe in it."

"I wasn't worried."

She touched his jaw with one hand, then lightly traced her fingertips over his face. He set her on the bed and backed off.

"Where are you?" she asked, sounding distressed.

"I'll be on the sofa. If you need anything, just yell."

"I want you...to stay."

The words were spoken so softly he barely heard them. "I can't," he said lightly. "I can't make promises on your safety if I do."

"Stay."

The word was a plea. He closed his eyes and tried to think of noble things—honor and all that. It didn't work. He took a step forward. A hand touched his thigh. He opened his eyes as she slipped both hands around his waist and leaned her head against his stomach. She moved her hands slowly up and down his back under the sweatshirt.

"I can't promise a platonic night if you keep that up."

Without a word, she slipped off her boots, then stood and removed the robe. His heart kicked into overdrive. She paused, her head tilted as if she listened for his movements. Her hands went to the buttons that ran down the front of the pajamas.

"Let me," he requested, his voice deeper as sexual need overrode scruples and all that baggage.

She dropped her hands to her sides, inviting him to finish the task. He was glad she couldn't see how his fingers trembled as he did. He pushed the fabric off her shoulders and tossed the top on a chair.

"Wait," he said, although she didn't move. He threw his sweat suit on the chair, then yanked his socks off. He noted her bare feet. "Now," he murmured and caught his thumbs in the waistband of her pajama bottoms. They slid easily down her slender hips and settled in a puddle on the floor. She stepped out of them.

Then she lifted her arms to him.

It was more than a mortal man could resist, and he had never claimed to be a saint. He stepped forward and felt her heat all along his body.

The words wouldn't be suppressed. "You're beautiful," he said, "so beautiful, it takes my breath away."

"That was a song," she said softly, pressing her

lips to his neck and causing lightning to flash into every part of him.

Before he moved to the bed, he made one more attempt at fair play. "Will you have regrets in the morning?"

She kissed along his collarbone. "I don't know. I guess we won't know until the sun comes up, will we?" she asked with perfect logic. "And by then it won't matter."

A shudder went through him. "No," he said and, letting her go, stepped back. "It's no deal. I won't exchange safety for sex."

He clenched his fists instead of reaching for her when he saw tears spring into her eyes. Her cheeks flushed deep red. He realized she was humiliated.

"I'm sorry," she said hoarsely. "I shouldn't have...of course you don't want...I'm sorry..." She gestured helplessly. "My clothes. Could you give them to me?"

There was no way he could leave it at that. With a groan he gathered her into his arms. "Little fool. Of course I want you. I don't sleep nights for dreaming of you. No moment of the day passes without thoughts of you. Dammit, I'm trying to be honorable toward you. You're vulnerable, and I shouldn't take advantage of that, but if you want me, then...I won't say no."

He dried the tears clinging to her lashes with his lips, then he moved softly down her face to her mouth. Her lips trembled under his as he touched them, then her arms slipped around his shoulders as she arched against him.

The last of his scruples fell away. Her touch ignited a need that wouldn't, couldn't be denied. Reasoning didn't even enter into the equation.

With a twist, he fell to the bed, taking her weight as she came down with him. Rolling to one side, he slipped a hand under her hair and held her head in position to deepen the kiss.

For a long time he only kissed her and caressed lightly along her back. Finally he had to have more or he'd explode with the force of his need for her. He slid his hands along her hips and stroked her buttocks, then the back of her thighs. He kissed her breasts and explored the texture of her delicately pink nipples. When he touched her leg and applied the gentlest pressure, she shifted it to one side, granting him access to all of her.

Shannon had never known passion could be so totally engrossing. The world narrowed to his room, his bed, the places where he caressed. Bright veils of red and blue flashed through her mental vision like magical draperies controlled by a genie.

When he touched her most intimately, she nearly cried out as sensation climbed to dangerously high levels.

"Please," she said, not sure what she was asking. "Please. Oh, yes!" she said on a moan of pleasure as he coaxed her toward the peak. "Rory, I need...I want you... Now, please. Now."

"Wait," Rory whispered hoarsely and rolled away

from her. He was near the edge. So was she. He fumbled in the bedside drawer and found one of the condoms he'd recently bought. Just in case. Yeah, right.

He quickly rolled it on and turned back to her. Her pupils were dilated with passion, and her eyes gleamed in the dim light from the lamp. A flush spread upward from her breasts to her cheeks. She once again reminded him of the confident young woman who had caught his attention on the street not long ago.

"How could I have taken so long to notice you?" he asked. "I was the blind one. Or stupid." He chuckled as he ran a fingertip from her forehead, over her nose, then down to the dewy valley between her breasts. "You are the most incredibly beautiful woman I've ever seen."

Shannon pressed fervent kisses on his throat and chest. Her incoherent thoughts flew to her tongue. "You make me feel that way. Beautiful. Sexy. Hot. Cold. Frightened."

He tipped her chin up with a hooked finger. "You don't ever have to be afraid of me," he told her fiercely. "Don't you know I'd do anything to keep you safe? Anything," he said, feeling humble and courageous at the same time.

She stirred too many things in him, this woman with her stubborn independence and her distrust of others that she seemed unaware of. He wanted to show her more than pleasure. He wanted...too many things. He couldn't begin to enumerate them.

"I know. I think I know," Shannon amended with a little confused shake of her head.

She didn't want words, not now. She wanted only him and all the things they made each other feel. When she touched him as intimately as he was touching her, he tensed, then bucked against her as she stroked up and down, driving him to the same madness as he did her. She carefully gathered the soft pouch in one hand and caressed it, then stroked the skin in back and front.

He rolled over her, taking his weight on his arms. She held her breath as he moved gently against her, ever so slowly pressing more deeply. He slid against her so that she was further aroused with each stroke. Her hips arced upward to meet each thrust as the need grew.

Rory knew the moment had come when he could take no more. He had to know all of her, every last sweet inch. She was moist and ready for him, her every move designed to drive him insane. He was nearly there.

With his last ounce of control, he rose and positioned himself, then slowly let gravity do the rest, sinking into her warm, womanly depths until they were completely merged at last. "Don't move," he warned.

"I want movement," she explained, so earnestly he nearly smiled. But then she thrust upward with a little twist that wrung a gasp from him. "I need more...more."

Everything faded into a red haze. He slid a hand

between them and caressed her until she went wild beneath him. When her ecstatic little cries faded to panting breaths, he let himself go, thrusting again and again until he was both sated and drained. And even then, he didn't want to stop.

Shannon felt his contractions deep within her own body, a strange, marvelous sensation that joined with the aftershocks of pleasure that surprised her as he continued to move deeply in her. When he was still, she sighed and lightly rubbed his back and shoulders.

"It was too marvelous," she said after a wonder-filled moment of contemplation. "I don't want it to end."

She felt his silent laughter before he moved to her side, taking her with him so they remained as one.

"Give me five minutes," he said.

Again she felt his soft laughter. She smiled, then yawned, suddenly too drowsy even to open her eyes. "Don't let go," she requested.

"I intend to hold you all night," he whispered.

"Be careful. That sounded like a promise."

"It was."

Rory kissed her rosy lips. He noticed the redness on her chin from his beard. He hadn't shaved that evening. But then, he hadn't been expecting company in his bed.

He glanced at the packet on the table. But he had prepared for whatever might happen, he admitted. He had known there would come a time when passion took over. And there would be no one there to stop them.

He just hadn't expected it to be quite like this. He hadn't wanted her to come to him from fear or need, but only from...what?

It was a question he wasn't ready to explore just yet. When? He couldn't answer that, either. Part of it depended on the woman who dozed peacefully—and trustfully if she but knew it—in his arms at this moment.

Tenderness, the strange, confusing tenderness that only she had ever aroused, surged through him. One thing was true. He would do anything to protect her from harm.

No one would hurt her. Not while there was life in his body.

With this thought, his body stirred. He began to move, surprised to find the need arising so soon. She made a sound of pleasure in her throat and began to move with him, urging him deeper, faster. The riptide of passion caught them up in its heady rush toward completion again and tossed them to a distant shore, far and away beyond anywhere he'd ever gone before. He knew it was the same for her.

Afterward she was silent.

"What are you thinking?" he asked.

She sighed. "It's just so powerful, passion is. I hadn't expected...I don't know what I expected."

He turned off the lamp and cupped his body around hers. "It's different," he admitted. But he didn't know why.

Chapter Eleven

Shannon rolled toward the light when she awoke. She blinked, but it didn't go away. She blinked again and sat up in bed.

Her brain moved with the speed of syrup on a cold morning, but finally she realized she really could make out the rectangle of light that was the window, and that it was morning.

Almost fearfully, she glanced around the room. She could detect dark gray outlines against lighter ones— a chest of drawers against one wall, a small table beside the bed, light sheets against the dark comforter.

"Dear God," she whispered, light-headed and not quite believing in this miracle. It could be a momentary fluke—

"Ah, you're up. Almost."

She turned toward the voice. An outline, definitely human and masculine, moved toward her. She was afraid to close her eyes, afraid the magic would disappear and she would be left in darkness again.

Eyes wide, she watched him stop by the bed and bend over. As his head came closer, she strained to see his features, but that was beyond her.

"Good morning," he murmured huskily, tenderly, with all the nuances of a well-pleased lover.

A tremor ran through her, reminding her of shared delight and all the other passions of the night. Mixed up with the memories was the miracle of the morning.

"I can see you," she said in a hoarse whisper.

He stopped, his face inches from hers. "Say that again."

"I can see...sort of. Shadows and outlines. I can see your head backlighted by the window. Your face isn't clear. It's like one of those store mannequins with indentations for eyes and just a suggestion of a nose and mouth, but I can tell it's a face."

He sat on the side of the bed. "I see," he said slowly, as if mulling over the implications.

"When I saw the light in the window, I thought it was a fluke, one of those odd flashes, more an impression of light than the reality of actually seeing it, but this time, it didn't go away when I blinked." She pressed her hands over her face. "I was so afraid it would."

He lifted her into his lap and held her close. "It's just the beginning of the miracle."

It wasn't until she felt the soft material of his sweatshirt against her breasts that she realized she didn't have a stitch of clothing on.

"My pajamas..." she began. Visions of the night raced through her mind, of him and her, of touching and kissing, of pleasure and contentment. "Oh."

Rory wasn't surprised that the miracle of her vision had come back this morning. It seemed in tune with the miracle of the night, of making love with this woman until the pleasure was almost too much to bear. That her sight should return now seemed to follow as naturally as day followed night.

"Yeah, *oh*," he teased lightly, although he felt almost humbled by all that had happened. "I'll get them for you in a minute. First, a shower."

As he stood with her cradled against his chest, he noticed the sheets. The strange tenderness came over him again. Stubborn, proud, independent—and a virgin.

He should have known that. Her hesitation and uncertainty, all were signs that pointed to her inexperience as a lover. He worried that he might have demanded too much of her during the night, but then, he hadn't been the only one making demands. Her hunger had been as great.

Taking a deep breath—now was not the time for passion—he carried her to the bathroom and, standing her on the mat, flipped on the water. He lathered his hands and washed her gently, ignoring her laughing protests and blushes when his touch became intimate.

"There's no part of you I don't already know," he reminded her, allowing himself one quick kiss.

He shampooed her hair, noticing the way the water subdued the fiery tones to dark auburn. Desire snipped at his self-control. He quickly washed, then dried them both. There were other things more important at this moment.

"Look in the mirror," he suggested and gently turned her in the right direction, then flicked on the row of lights at each side. He turned the blow-dryer on.

Shannon blinked in the brighter light, then leaned closer. She could make out two shapes. His and hers. She stared and stared, wanting to see more, but deliriously happy to recognize shapes and forms, as he dried her hair.

"Toothbrush," he said and put it in her hand.

She held it and stared at the vague line in her hand. "It's such a miracle," she said in wonder.

"Nah," he said casually, "it's just a toothbrush. Been around hundreds of years."

She smiled at his humor, knowing he was giving her time to become accustomed to the wonder of seeing the world again, however vaguely. When they were dressed, she in the pink pajamas and robe and a pair of his tube socks, he escorted her to the kitchen.

"Breakfast is nearly ready," he said. "Sausage and eggs and toast okay?"

"Yes."

He came to her. "Coffee." He set the cup on the table.

She stared at the dark shape against the lighter tones of the table. "Is the table white?" she asked.

"Yes. Badly chipped, though. It's oak underneath. I'm going to remove the paint and leave it natural. When I get around to it."

His laughter warmed her all the way through. She followed his movements as he fried eggs and buttered toast. In a few minutes he came to the table with two plates and silverware. She tingled when he brushed her arm.

He touched her shoulder lightly. "Eat up."

She did, finding she was ravenous. In more ways than one, she mused, aware of his presence in ways she'd never been aware of the male of the species. Her life had always been too busy, too focused on her goals, to notice things other women seemed to take for granted.

Being without sight had forced her to slow down and smell the roses, so to speak. Recalling the passion of the night, she wanted to make love with him again, but, as usual when morning came, other problems loomed.

"Regrets?"

The question caused her to jump guiltily. "No," she said firmly. "Not exactly." She sighed. "The morning casts a new light on the situation, so to speak."

"Because you can see?" His tone was harder.

She considered. "No. Because last night complicates things between us. Sex is, or can be, a form of bonding. Have you ever heard of the Stockholm Syndrome?''

''No.'' He was clearly surprised at the question.

''Well, briefly, it's what happens when a captive identifies with her captors. In the States, the Patty Hearst case was an example. It's a survival tactic—to become one with the others, to fit in. That way, you won't be singled out to be punished or tortured.''

''If last night was torture, darlin', I can take a lot more of it.''

Heat crawled up her neck as she thought of his caresses—and her own. She doggedly continued with her explanation. ''Something of the same thing can happen when people go through a traumatic event together, or a person saves another's life. A bond is established. That isn't necessarily bad, but it can lead to complications neither want. Later, it may be hard to break off when…when they realize it was a mistake.''

After a long minute, he asked, ''Which am I—the captor or the captivated?'' His brief laugh was sardonic.

She didn't miss the inference of the last word. ''I think we were both caught in circumstances beyond our control. The shooting, your finding me, the loss of sight, being neighbors, my worries about the man in the truck. It all adds up.''

''To last night?''

She nodded. ''You're a naturally protective and caring person—''

''Spare me the psychoanalysis. Last night may

have been triggered by circumstances, but what happened...that had been building for days, since you got out of the hospital.''

"But it wasn't real. Don't you see?''

"More than you think.''

There was a tinge of bitterness in his voice. She tried to analyze it, but too many impressions of him, and the night, swirled around in her mind. "The passion, with everything else, is too confusing,'' she tried to explain. She sighed. "I'd like for us to be friends.''

"But not lovers,'' he concluded.

She forced herself to nod.

"We can try it.''

His agreement didn't ring quite true. As if he didn't believe they could be merely friends.

Looking toward the bright rectangles of light, she reflected on the miracle of sight and of love. They were gifts people often took for granted. Tears filled her eyes before she could will them away. Keeping her head down, she quickly finished the meal and thanked her host.

"I need to go home so you can get ready for work. It's Friday, isn't it?'' She rose, then remembered her shoes. "My boots.'' She tried to recall where she'd pulled them off.

"I'll get them.''

He helped her into them, then went home with her. They checked the house and found it empty. She thanked him, then waited for him to leave. Her emotional control shaky, she wanted to be alone, to think about where she was and where she was going from here. It wasn't possible with him around.

"I know an eye specialist in Denver," Rory said, standing by the door, reluctant to leave although she wanted him to be gone. "You should have a checkup. If you like, I'll make an appointment and drive you down."

She hesitated, then asked, "Can we wait? I'd like more time to see what happens."

"All right. Let me know when."

Returning to his place, he reflected on the irony of life. He'd tried not to take advantage of Shannon, to be honorable and all that, but last night, when she'd come to him, the hunger had been too much for both of them. This morning, her sight back to some degree, she'd withdrawn from him with some story about captive syndromes. It wasn't what he'd expected.

But when had the beautiful lady cop ever done what the heck was expected?

Well, their problems would have to wait until they got a moment alone. Which might be a while.

He sighed, pocketed his wallet, left a note on the table for his dad and stepmother and hurried off to work. If he was lucky, they wouldn't stay for more than the weekend.

Huh, he'd never had that kind of luck.

Shannon dressed, then called Megan and Kate and told them she thought her vision was returning. "It's like walking through the house at twilight without any lights on, very shadowy, but not impossible."

"We've got to celebrate," Kate declared after a spate of excited questions and discussion of the possibilities. "Come over for dinner tonight. We'll have champagne. I'll send Jess over to pick you up. Oh, Shannon, this is such good news!"

Smiling pensively, Shannon hung up, feeling much better after talking to her cousins. She picked up a catalog and peered at it, but the print was beyond her. She knew she was letting her expectations build too much, too fast, but it was hard not to.

Like last night with Rory.

Flames swept over her at the memory. He had been so wonderful, passionate and tender and all the things a woman could desire. And yet, she'd wanted more.

What?

It was a question she wasn't ready to answer. Not just yet. There were so many elements in her life that she needed to sort through. One was the miracle of the morning. Would it last? If it didn't, then what?

It was a question she couldn't quite face at this moment when her emotions ran from extreme hope that she would soon be completely well to abysmal fear that the darkness would return.

She walked through the house and was able to discern each piece of furniture. Remembering that the doctor hadn't wanted her to strain her eyes after he removed the bandages, she put on the sunglasses again. Her vision seemed to go dark. Panicky, she jerked them off.

It was okay. She could still see.

Tucking the glasses into her shirt pocket, she decided to wear them only when she went outside. In a flurry of energy, she cleaned the whole house and polished the furniture. An odd thing, especially since housework wasn't high on her priorities. When she finished, she truly felt at home in her new place.

Napping on the sofa that afternoon, she woke when she heard a car on the road. She tensed, but it wasn't a vehicle she recognized. It slowed, then turned in at Rory's house.

Probably a rancher with a sick dog. The demands on a vet's time were as great as those for a human doctor.

Curious, she went to the window. The sun caused her to flinch. She put the glasses on. Hmm, there was a car at his place, but she couldn't detect anyone— no, wait.

She yanked the sunglasses off, shaded her eyes and stared as hard as she could. Someone was walking from the house to the car. Now they were walking back. Another person came outside and met the first. They had been inside the house.

Her breath quick and uneven, she called information, got the number of Rory's office, then decided to call Jess instead. He was at his desk. She explained what was happening.

"I'll check it out," he promised.

Relieved, she made sure her doors were locked, then considered getting her handgun from the suitcase in the closet. Remembering the World War II binoculars that had belonged to her great-uncle, she retrieved them and went to the window.

The scene next door jumped into view. A man was carrying something into the house, not out of it. Suitcases, she realized. Oh, no! Rory apparently had company.

She called Jess back, but he was out of the office. She hoped he and the sheriff didn't come roaring up the road, sirens blasting.

No such luck.

She heard the siren less than a minute later. She also heard Rory's truck arrive. She sighed and made her way out the back door and across to the other house. She knocked on the door and waited.

Rory answered. "Hi, come on in. There seems to be some excitement at this end of the county," he mentioned wryly.

"It's my fault," she admitted, going into the kitchen. "I saw someone at your house, so I called the cops."

"That was kind of you. Let me introduce you to my dad and stepmother." He took her arm.

"Uh, maybe another time—"

The vehicle with the siren arrived and turned in the drive. Shannon heard another vehicle stop. Jess had sent two cruisers, she surmised. She groaned in embarrassment.

"And more company," Rory murmured. "Come on in, sheriff, Jess," he called. "The door's open."

"What's going on?"

A woman's voice, very irritated. His stepmother, no doubt. Shannon wished she could crawl into a hole.

"A surprise visit by Wind River's finest," Rory answered the woman, amusement underlying the statement.

"Is everything okay?" she heard Jess ask as the two lawmen stepped inside the narrow hall.

A form separated itself from the others and came to her. "You okay?"

She recognized the voice and the shape—six feet six inches, two hundred and forty pounds. Her boss, the sheriff of the county. "Yes. Everything is fine. False alarm." She smiled faintly.

"I forgot to tell Shannon my folks were due in today," Rory said casually, as if it were her business to know. "Dad, Catherine, this is Shannon Bannock, my next-door neighbor. Her cousin, Detective Jess Fargo. And the sheriff. Gene, you probably remember my dad, Richard Daniels, and my stepmother, don't you?"

"Sure. How you doing?"

The men shook hands while Shannon and the stepmother murmured greetings. Rory offered them coffee, but Jess and Gene said they had to get back to the office.

After they left, Shannon backed toward the kitchen. "I've got to run, too. Sorry to have distressed you, Mrs. Daniels. I hope you enjoy your visit."

She turned and ran smack into a warm chest. Rory's arms closed around her. "Easy," he murmured.

"You should watch where you're going," Mrs. Daniels suggested pointedly.

Heat flamed in Shannon's cheeks. She tried to pull away from Rory, but he wouldn't let her go.

"She would, but she's blind as a bat." His tone was level, but Shannon sensed the underlying anger and coldness directed at the other woman.

A beat of silence followed this declaration.

"Where're your glasses, darling?" Rory continued, anger roiling in him like a dormant volcano coming to life. "You probably should wear them until we get you checked out. Some of her vision seems to be returning," he explained to the other two. He plucked the shades from her pocket and slid them on her face. "There," he said. "Why don't we all go out to dinner tonight?"

Shannon shook her head. "I already have plans. Kate is going to have me over."

"And she didn't include me? I'll have to speak to her about that. Come on, I'll walk you home, then I have to get back to work. Be back in a sec," he told his folks. He took Shannon's hand and led the way to her house.

"I'm really sorry," she said as they crossed the bridge. "I upset your mother—"

"My stepmother. And I don't give a damn how upset she gets."

He was aware of the quick study Shannon directed his way. He didn't know if she could see it, but he smiled to show he wasn't angry with her.

"You and she don't get along?"

"We manage. My father loves her and she appears

to make him happy. That's all that's important to me. Step up.''

They were on the porch. He reluctantly halted there, knowing he had to go do his duty to his guests. ''Thanks for watching out for me. I appreciate it.''

''Right. Nothing like calling the cops on your relatives to make them feel welcome.''

He laughed, the day suddenly seeming much brighter than it had that morning. ''I sleep much better knowing there's a cop next door. Of course, it's even better when she's in my bed, but—''

Shannon's stifled gasp and reproving frown didn't do a thing to quell the hunger that surged through him.

''How about dinner tomorrow night? You can help me entertain to make up for today,'' he suggested, liking that idea. ''I'm not going to take no for an answer.''

She burst into laughter, surprising and enchanting him. ''That gives me a lot of choice, but since I guess I owe you for today, I'll graciously accept.''

Unable to resist, he leaned over and kissed her tempting lips. ''I wish we were alone.''

She kept her hands between them, lightly restraining him when he would have taken the kiss deeper. He sighed and backed off. ''See you later.''

''Tomorrow,'' she corrected.

''Yeah, tomorrow.'' He retraced his steps.

Catherine was waiting for him at the door. ''Your father has decided to lie down and rest,'' she informed him in chilly tones. "There's only one bed in the house. I put him on the sofa."

Rory cursed silently at the glance she gave him. He'd forgotten about the bed. "I'll set up a bed in one of the guest rooms. I meant to do it yesterday but, uh, other things got in the way."

He retreated to the guest room and proceeded to put the bed together. His stepmother followed. He returned to his room, stripped the sheets and carried the mattress, then the springs to the other bed.

"The new set I ordered hasn't arrived yet," he explained, all at once enjoying the disapproval on Catherine's face. She looked as if she'd swallowed a sour gnat. He tried to restrain a smile.

"You seem to be quite cozy with your neighbor," she prodded, trying to ferret information out of him.

Okay, he could comply. He beamed an innocent smile at his stepmom, who was fourteen years older than his thirty-two years and twenty years younger than his father.

"Shannon. Yes. She's my fiancée, although we haven't announced it yet. She wants to tell her family first. I suppose it's all right for you and Dad to know, though."

"Fiancée?"

He enjoyed the shock that spread across the carefully made-up but relatively unlined face. His stepmother was a good-looking woman. Her pants outfit was perfectly tailored to her model-thin frame and probably cost as much as his whole wardrobe. Or Shannon's.

Warmth speared through him at the thought of
Shannon as he fetched clean sheets and blankets and
made up the bed. "Yes. We decided last night to
make it official. You can be the very first to wish us
well."

Her face darkened. "I don't recall you mentioning
this person previously. Have you thought about how
it would be, living with a blind person?"

The anger neared the boiling point. "No, but I've
thought about how it would be living with Shannon."

The look he gave her must have been convincing.
She backed up a step. "I suppose you know what
you're doing. Men always think they do," she said
as a parting shot before going into the living room
and telling his father the bed was ready.

Rory suppressed the fury with an effort and headed
for his truck. He had two surgeries that afternoon before he would be free, then he thought he would go
for a long walk before facing dinner with his relatives.

When he arrived at the office, he had a few
minutes. Picking up the phone, he dialed Shannon's
number. "Hi," he said when she answered. "I
thought I'd better warn you. We got engaged last
night. I had to confess all to my stepmother this morning. She suspected we were more than friends, so I
satisfied her curiosity about you."

He smiled at the silence on the end of the line.

"Are you insane?" she finally asked.

"Crazy about you," he teased, the anger mysteri-
ously gone as soon as he heard her voice. He could

almost hear the wheels turning as she thought things through.

"Did I leave earrings or something beside your bed and your stepmother found them?"

"Something like that," he admitted ruefully, then added quickly, "She saw me kiss you goodbye."

"Huh?"

He smiled. She was definitely annoyed.

"Because of a kiss, we had to become engaged?" she questioned in disbelief. "What is this—a throwback to the Victorian age?"

"Yep. Believe me, with Catherine, it's the only way." He waited, giving her time to think it through in the straightforward manner that pleased him. A man could do worse than hook up with a woman like her. She had sense as well as courage.

She sighed. "How long will this go on? Am I supposed to inform my family?"

"Knowing my stepmother, that might be a good idea."

"Okay. Let me know when we become disengaged."

"Right."

After they hung up, he thought about it. He wasn't sure there was a time limit on engagements, and if so, what came next? Warmth flowed through him as several suggestions came to mind.

Her new little cousin, Mandy, met Shannon at the door when she arrived with Jess. "I'm the VIP in my class," Mandy announced. "I got to lead when we marched all around the room to the music."

"Wow, VIP," Shannon said, lifting the four-year-old and giving her a kiss. "You were probably the best one they ever had."

"Yes," Mandy agreed happily.

"Don't be braggy," Jeremy, her older brother, advised.

Mandy cast him a complacent glance. "Okay."

Shannon, as part of her family services tasks with the sheriff's department, had placed Mandy with Kate last June. Kate and Jess had married and then adopted the child. Under her new family's loving care, the orphan was blossoming.

Kate greeted Shannon with a hug. "How's your sight?"

"Still with me. I've been staring at stuff all day. I even tried to watch a soap this afternoon, but all I could see were flickers across the screen."

"Hmm. Jess tells me you called the cops on your neighbor this morning."

Shannon admitted she had. "His dad and stepmom, to be exact. I was so embarrassed."

Kate's family thought that was hilarious. "Have you heard the mysterious truck out your way again?" Jess asked.

"What mysterious truck?" Kate demanded.

Jess explained about the stranger.

Shannon assured her cousin it was nothing. "Just an overactive imagination on my part. There's probably a very innocent explanation for it all."

"Ha!" was Kate's reaction. "Maybe you should stay over here for a while."

"I'm fine. Really."

"Rory's keeping an eye on her," Jess assured his wife.

"Ohh, the heartthrob of the county," Kate teased.

"Uh, I have some other news."

Instant silence fell on the group.

"Rory and I are engaged. Sort of." She couldn't help but laugh as the silence lengthened.

"You and Rory?" Kate finally said, sounding like a frog with a sore throat.

"Apparently his stepmother is kind of nosy and was asking about me—on account of my calling the cops, I suspect—anyway, he told her we were engaged. When he called to inform me of this fact, I told him I would go along with the story."

"Maybe you really will marry." This from Kate.

"Can I be your flower girl?" Mandy requested.

"Well, well, well," Jess murmured.

"I don't have to be in the wedding, do I?" Jeremy asked with an anxious expression.

Shannon felt her face grow warm. Her family was taking this much too seriously, she feared. "I'm helping out a neighbor, that's all. Rory and I are just friends."

And lovers, the part of her that was painfully truthful added. She held on to her smile with an effort and hoped Rory's evening was proving as difficult as hers.

Later that evening, after Jess had dropped her at home, Shannon heard a familiar step on the back porch.

"It's Rory," he called out.

She unlocked the door, her heart going into overdrive. "What is it?"

"Nothing. This," he corrected.

She received the briefest of warnings as his hands closed on her shoulders. Then his mouth claimed hers in a kiss that was gentle but hinted at passion kept on a tight leash.

"Don't," she said reprovingly when she could speak. Fatigue pounded through her, causing a headache.

"I had to come over and tell my fiancée goodnight," he explained. "What did you tell your family about us?"

"The truth."

"As in?"

"That we were pretending to be engaged because of something to do with your stepmother."

He groaned, then rested his forehead against hers and chuckled. "Must you be so perversely honest? Kate called and told me she would have Jess break every bone in my body if you ended up hurt."

Shannon was at a loss for words. "They worry about me," she finally said.

"What about me?" he demanded softly, nuzzling along her temple. "What about my heart?"

Before she could think of a reply, he gave her a hug, then left after reminding her to lock the door. She went to bed, but it was a long time before the churning inside settled enough for her to sleep.

In her dreams someone kept asking what it all meant.

"Nothing," she told the invisible person over and over. "We're not in love. I'm being a good neighbor, that's all."

Chapter Twelve

The phone started ringing at nine the next morning.
Shannon discovered the news of her and Rory's engagement was in the local paper. After the fifth call,
she dialed his office and asked to speak to him.

"Hi, darling," he said, as chirpy as a robin with
its first worm of the day, when he came on the line.

"Don't you 'darling' me," she snapped.

"Ah, you've heard about the news in the paper."

"Yes. Did you—"

"No, I didn't. I suspect my dear stepmother was
the culprit."

"Why?" Shannon asked, totally perplexed. "Why
would she do something like that?"

"To put me in an awkward position. She didn't

believe the engagement story. I thought I was very convincing.''

Shannon huffed in exasperation. "If your story was some kind of misguided attempt to protect my reputation, I would prefer to be consulted before any more acts of gallantry.''

"Right," he agreed easily. "I've got a patient waiting. See you tonight. Wear that black outfit. It's a knockout.''

Shannon hung up, not sure whether to be annoyed or resigned at the turn of events. Resigned, she decided. She would have to continue the engagement farce now that he had started them down that slippery slope, at least until his relatives left.

For a moment, she considered what it might be like to really be engaged to him.

If he loved her. If she loved him.

Her heart skidded out of control, echoing off the walls of her chest like the rabid beat of a mad drummer.

Funny how you could know a person all your life, but not really know them. Rory was a wonderful person—kind, humorous, exciting…

Yes, it would be easy, very easy, to fall for her handsome neighbor.

Suddenly despondent, she put on the dark glasses, dressed warmly and ventured outside, needing air and space around her. When she looked at the nearest peaks, she noticed how blue the sky was that highlighted them—

Blue!

She leaned on the rail fence while excitement danced through her. She could see color! Eagerly she scanned the sky. The color stayed, only a spot in the center of her vision, true, but still…

She should call Rory and tell him…no, he was busy, she remembered. But today was Saturday. He would be home by noon. She would tell him then.

Returning to the house, she went around peering at things—the pictures on the walls, the clock on the mantel, the print in the sofa cushions. Her gaze fell on the department store catalog. With hands that trembled, she picked it up and stared at the cover.

Taking it with her, she went to her bedroom and retrieved her prescription glasses. The printing went from fuzzy to sharp. The flesh tones, the red outfit the model was wearing, all became clear when she held the catalog within a foot of her nose and gazed directly at the cover, although the edges stayed dark and fuzzy.

She had tunnel vision, she realized. Which was much better than no vision at all.

Breathing jerkily, she put one hand over her right eye. The vision in the injured eye was dim, but she could still see. With the left eye covered, the images were clear and in color and only a little fuzzy around the edges.

Her eyes were continuing to improve, *both* of them. Rory had been right! The miracle was just beginning. She hugged herself and wished he were there. She needed him…no!

No, she merely wanted to share the news with him.

Regaining her composure, she went to her office. She picked up a page of notes, studied it, then turned the computer on. Smiling, filled with eager anticipation, she got to work.

Shannon put the finishing touches on her makeup. Her insides felt like a quivering bowl of tapioca as she put on eye shadow and blush and lipstick. When Rory knocked, then called out her name upon entering, she nearly jumped out of her skin.

"Coming," she called, grabbing her purse. She joined him in the kitchen.

"Hey, pretty lady," he said, appreciation in his voice.

She stopped before him and stared. Reaching up, she touched his handsome face and ran her fingertips over the strong planes and bone structure.

He held still, his eyes—his *blue* eyes—on her face, their expression solemn and slightly puzzled.

She traced a line over each dark eyebrow. "Your eyes are blue," she said in a near whisper. "Your hair is black. So are your eyelashes. You have a tiny scar here, just under your jaw."

"You can see that?" he asked quietly.

"Better, but not perfectly. Tunnel vision, but with color," she explained.

His smile flashed. His teeth were white and even, contrasting brilliantly with his tanned face. Her heart clenched as she acknowledged how very handsome her pretend fiancé actually was.

The next thing she knew, he'd caught her around

the waist and lifted her off her feet. He swung her around and around until she was dizzy and laughing and wonderfully happy. Then, while the world continued to spin, he kissed her laughter into silence and the happiness spiraled into a glow that lit her from the inside out.

His lips were warm and supple on hers. The kiss was tender as well as passionate. It lasted a long time.

"We have to go," he finally said.

If he loved her. If she loved him.

The words swirled through her mind, and she wished they could stay here, alone, and not have to deal with the world at this moment. Subdued, she reached for her coat.

He held the down jacket for her, zipped it, then handed her the matching mittens. Tucking her hand into his arm, he guided her over the bridge to his house.

"I thought you said our reservation was at seven," his stepmother greeted them impatiently.

"It is," Rory replied evenly. "We have plenty of time."

As the woman walked past her, Shannon glimpsed her face. Catherine had large eyes—dark brown, perhaps—and short, blond-highlighted hair. She was slender and very beautiful in a sophisticated way that Shannon could never hope to match. She seemed to hold a grudge against Rory.

On the hour-long drive, Rory and she rode in the back seat of his father's car while his stepmom drove and his father took the passenger side. Once at the restaurant, Shannon tried to relax, but found herself increasingly nervous around his family.

Catherine kept up a stream of social chatter about the changes in the town over the years. "Perhaps it'll get some good restaurants now that the resort is completed," she said, "and people won't have to drive all the way down to the interstate highway to get a decent meal."

"I've always liked the café in town," Shannon said, compelled to defend her home turf.

There was the tiniest pause, then Rory laid his hand over hers. "Me, too. It offers a variety of vegetables that you don't get in fancy places like this. A person soon tires of baked potatoes and salads."

Catherine shuddered delicately. "I recall the time Richard took me there. They had prepared dried beans and cooked greens with globs of bacon fat in them."

That effectively killed the topic of discussion. When a small combo set up and started playing some slow, dreamy numbers, the stepmother stood.

"I'd like to dance," she said, her eyes going from her husband to Rory.

Shannon was decidedly uncomfortable with the woman's manner, which was very demanding. She carefully kept a neutral expression when Rory stood.

He clasped her arm. Shannon shot him a startled glance when he urged her to her feet. "Come on, Dad," he said with mock forbearance. "The ladies want to dance. We can shuffle them around the floor to the slow tunes."

In a moment, Shannon was snuggled against Rory on the crowded dance floor.

"Ahh," he murmured, as if he found this deeply satisfying. "I missed you last night."

She thought of his arms, of the way he'd kissed and caressed her, of the excitement of his lovemaking. *If he loved her.*

She wished she'd stop thinking that. It made her hurt inside. "This isn't very smart," she began on a light note.

He rested his cheek against her temple. "No lectures tonight, please. Let's enjoy the evening. As much as we can," he added wryly.

"Why do you dislike your stepmother?"

Shannon felt the muscles in his shoulders tighten for a second before he shrugged. "I find her hard to take."

"She's very beautiful."

"No, she isn't," he corrected. "You are."

Warmth spread all through her as she looked up. Their eyes met and held. Shannon, though limited in vision and experience, knew passion when she saw it. His hunger engulfed her until she was consumed by an equal need.

"I never knew passion could be like this," she said, bewildered by the fire and the sweet, wild temptation of his touch. For all her studies in human nature, nothing had prepared her for it—the yearning, the pounding heart, the delight and anticipation and misery. "I don't understand why it happens or how. Why me? Why you? Why now?"

"Because it's the right time, the right place and the right people." He smiled at her. "We're right together."

He made it sound so simple, but the intensity of his gaze said it wasn't. They were both caught in the force of their mutual hunger, driven relentlessly like tumbleweeds before the wind.

Someone bumped her. Shannon gazed into cold eyes that were expertly made up to enhance the seductive allure in them. She felt the woman's dislike as a palpable thing—a chill all the way to the soul. The stepmother did not wish her well. She couldn't figure out why.

"The band is quite good, isn't it?" the woman said, her calculating gaze going to Rory.

"Yes," he answered briefly.

His face was devoid of emotion. Shannon felt the struggle between the other two—the woman's advance, his retreat. With expert skill, he glided them away from the older couple.

"She wants you to like her," Shannon told him on a sudden insight, feeling sorry for the stepmother.

"She tried to seduce me when I was a teenager," he said. "I tolerate her for my father's sake, but I don't have to like her."

"Maybe you misread her intentions. Maybe she's sorry and wants to start over."

"Maybe."

He was silent and tense the rest of the dance. Shannon missed the intensity, the excitement of knowing he wanted her that had been evident in his eyes. He had closed her out. She found she didn't like it any more than the other woman did.

With an effort, she made polite conversation the rest of the evening and ate the artfully prepared meal. Rory, too, chatted amiably, but she sensed the strain in him as the hours wore on.

''I heard on the news you've been having a series of robberies in the county,'' his father said. ''Someone broke into a store in town a couple of weeks after the...uh, the gas-station incident.''

Rory nodded. ''It's worrisome. Other than some rustling, we've never had much serious crime in these parts.'' He chuckled unexpectedly. ''Remember that time you surprised a burglar trying to get in the house?''

Mr. Daniels laughed, too, sounding very much like his son. However, Shannon noticed the older man's eyes were dark in color. Father and son didn't favor each other.

She wondered if Rory took after his mother's side of the family and if that contributed to his stepmother's animosity toward him. Perhaps she feared the son reminded the father of his first wife?

Sometimes, Shannon knew from her studies, a person used jealousy as a tool to alienate others from each other. That person became the eye of a storm of her own making, all attention revolving around her. Was his stepmother, in her own insecurity, driving a wedge between father and son?

As Rory drew his father out about chasing the burglar all over the neighborhood dressed only in skivvies, with a butcher knife in hand, she realized something else. Rory cared for his father and, in his kindness toward the older man, tried to be tolerant of his father's wife. He just refused to play her mind games.

It came to Shannon that she could help. She suspected Rory had thought of the engagement as a way to deflect his stepmom's demand for attention. Since she'd agreed to the deception, she could at least play her part.

After they had all declined dessert, she laid her hand on Rory's shoulder and playfully tickled the back of his neck. "Darling, do you think we could go? I'm rather tired after the excitement of the morning."

He studied her without answering, as if he'd forgotten the question while he contemplated her intimate gesture.

"What excitement?" Catherine demanded.

"I've regained more of my sight. I can see color now. With my new glasses, I can even focus on things as long as they're right in front of my nose. I probably overdid it, but I worked on my notes all day."

"Shannon is going into family therapy as a psychologist," Rory explained to the other couple. "She only has to write the dissertation to finish her Ph.D."

Catherine frowned. "You said she was a police officer."

"She was…is. She was shot in the line of duty, stopping the robbery at the gas station. Didn't I tell you she was a heroine?"

His frank admiration added to the glow within. Shannon caressed his lean cheek. "And he was my hero. He saved my life by slowing the bleeding until the medics arrived."

"You were both lucky," Mr. Daniels declared. "You probably saved his life by showing up before he did—otherwise, he might have walked into the store and been shot. At least you could defend yourself," he said to Shannon.

"If you're ready?" Rory broke in, taking her hand and effectively changing the subject. He called for their coats while he took care of the bill.

Shannon was silent on the way home. So was her companion, who placed an arm around her shoulders when she shivered in the frigid air of the car. She was aware of him in every nerve, as if she had radar that tracked his every move. Once he leaned close and lightly kissed her on the temple. She stole a glance at him. His eyes returned her stare with the intensity she'd seen earlier.

His gaze flicked to the front seat, then back to her. He smiled, bent his head and kissed her. Then he smiled again and pressed her head to his shoulder, a smoldering promise in his eyes.

She wondered what she'd unleashed by acting the smitten fiancée. She was scared of the emotions that struggled just under the surface of her consciousness. Part of her wanted to abandon caution and accept the passion. For tonight, for this moment, that's what the rest of her wanted, too.

* * *

Shannon and her erstwhile fiancé led the way into Rory's house. He stopped abruptly when they entered the kitchen.

"What the hell?" he muttered.

She glanced around the large, comfortable room. Even she could see that it had been ransacked. Drawers were on the floor, their contents strewn about.

"What in the world?" his father said behind her.

"Someone has vandalized the place," she said. "Please stay where you are and don't touch anything. Rory, call Jess. He'll need to investigate."

Rory put in the call. In less than ten minutes, Kate's husband arrived, followed a couple of minutes later by a young detective who brought a fingerprint kit and other crime-detection tools. They found some partial prints, but nothing they could use. The lock on the front door was broken. That's how entry had been made.

"Okay," Jess said an hour later, "we're through. You might want to check your belongings and see if anything is missing. I'll need to put it in my report."

Mrs. Daniels reported five hundred dollars was gone from her suitcase, plus a gold chain with a diamond pendant. Mr. Daniels had left his watch on the dresser. It, too, was missing. Shannon felt vaguely as if she were somehow at fault for not protecting their property. The culprit could have been the robber who'd shot her.

She covered a yawn, then held her wrist close to her face, trying to make out the tiny digital display.

"It's midnight," Rory told her. "Come on. I'll walk you home."

"I'll come with you," Jess, who'd been preparing to leave, volunteered. "We'll stick around a minute," he told the other detective.

The hair stood up on Shannon's neck when she entered her kitchen and flicked on the light. It, too, was a mess.

"I'll get the kit," the young detective said, coming in behind the other three.

Shannon shook her head. "I can't believe this. We've never had any trouble at all on the ranch. It's too far out for criminals to find the place."

Except for the robber who shot her. He knew where she lived. A tremor ran through her, as if she felt a malevolent force surrounding the place and extending to her neighbor's house as well.

Surprisingly, only the kitchen was vandalized. When Jess and his helper finished—nothing was missing as far as she could tell—the chief lawman turned to her. "You want to come stay with us for a while? I don't like the idea of your being alone here."

She thought of Kate, Jeremy and Mandy. She wasn't going to put her relatives in danger. Shaking her head, she told him she would be fine. "I really need to work on my notes. Besides, no crook hits the same place twice."

"She won't be alone," Rory said grimly. "She can stay with me."

There was a beat of silence, then Shannon smiled

in his direction. "That's kind of you, but you already have enough company—"

"You're right. I'll stay over here."

"Good," Jess said.

Shannon decided not to argue the point in front of the detectives. Jess, seemingly satisfied with this arrangement, bade them good-night.

Alone, she spoke to Rory. "You don't have to stay. I'll be fine."

He ignored her statement. "I'll go tell the folks and nail the front door closed." He gave a snort of laughter. "It would have been simpler to leave the door open."

This last was a reference to her place. She'd forgotten to lock up. The thief had waltzed right in.

"Yeah, it saves wear and tear on your doors," she quipped. "Really, you don't have to stay—"

"Yes, I do," he said quietly.

She didn't argue. She'd seen enough of him to know that it was his nature to protect and defend. That he was also stubborn went without saying.

Picking up the mess, she tried to ignore the hard thud of her heart and the increasing glow deep within. She was finishing the last drawer when he returned.

"We got my place straightened up," he reported. "All is back to normal."

"Except for the money and the missing items."

"A small price to pay. Here, let me put that up." He replaced the drawer and looked around. "How about a cup of hot chocolate? I'm too wired to sleep yet."

So was she. After putting the two mugs of milk in the microwave to heat, she retrieved a set of sheets from the linen closet and went to the guest bedroom. He followed her.

"Will we need another bed?" he asked huskily, his voice sending waves of longing spiraling through her.

She faced him. "I don't know."

"The ever-candid lady cop," he said softly. He crossed the floor, but stopped without touching her. "I won't lie or pretend I don't want you, but neither will I push you into anything you don't want."

She thought of the morning and the regrets that would surely follow. "You're dangerous to my peace of mind," she murmured, pressing a hand to her temple, the tender scar tissue reminding her that the scars of the heart could be more painful than those on the body.

"As you are to mine," he admitted.

She managed a smile. "Mutual madness."

"Yes."

He waited. She felt his patience, his tacit acceptance of her decision, whatever it was. It made her ache down deep where her dreams had once lived.

"It would be easier if you seduced me," she told him, only half joking.

"I want you, but I believe in playing fair. If it's wrong for you, then it's wrong for both of us."

"There are complications," she reminded him.

He didn't deny it.

She inhaled sharply, knowing she was stalling, not

quite able to refuse the harsh longing between them, not quite ready to surrender to it.

"Let's go have that chocolate," he suggested.

When he walked out and down the hall, she followed more slowly. He placed the mugs on the table and joined her there when she took her seat.

"You think the vandal was the man who shot you," he said as if reading her mind.

She nodded. "Yes. There's no evidence, but the feeling is so strong. It's as if I can sense his presence."

"I always follow my hunches." He took her hand and linked their fingers together. "Like now."

When his mouth met hers in a soft kiss, she felt the power of it down to her toes as need and passion, mixed in equal parts, collided within.

Passion she could handle. It was the need that frightened her. She drew back.

He watched her for a minute. "What scares you about us, about this?" he asked.

"It would be easy to fall in love...to think we were falling in love..."

"How do you know it won't happen, that it hasn't already happened?" he questioned softly.

"I won't let it," she said and heard the desperation. "We couldn't possibly be so foolish."

"I'm not like your father, Shannon. I can't account for what other people do, but for myself, I believe in fidelity. I would be faithful to my vows."

"It isn't that." She tried to laugh. "This conversation is getting awfully serious."

He brought her hand to his lips and pressed a kiss on the back of it, then into the palm. "I have something for you." He put a ring on her finger.

She stared at the small diamond set in a band of gold with an ivy pattern embossed on it.

"My mother's," he continued. "Luckily the thief didn't find it. I thought we should make our engagement official."

"I'm sure that's not necessary."

"Believe me, it is."

Recalling the stepmother's demanding attitude, Shannon reluctantly agreed. Drawing her hand from his, she said, "I'll wear it, but only until they leave."

"Good." He picked up the cup and took a sip. "It's late. I suppose we should go to bed."

He laughed suddenly, surprising her. She tried to make out the expression in his eyes, but saw only humor.

"I'll take the guest room. Odd, but now that we're officially engaged, I feel compelled to be honorable about the whole thing."

"Then your intentions weren't honorable the other night?" she asked, relieved at the lighter tone.

"Let's say they're under a state of constant review."

Which told her exactly nothing.

He pushed her cup toward her hand. "Drink up. Morning is going to come early, I suspect."

The clock struck one as she climbed into bed. It felt vast and lonely. She fought the need to go to him, knowing he would be gentle and welcoming. She touched the ring on her left hand. Her eyes burned with sudden tears.

She'd done a foolish thing, she realized, and had no one to blame but herself. She'd fallen in love with Rory.

And she'd walked into it with both eyes wide open.

Chapter Thirteen

Kate glanced pointedly at Shannon's left hand. "Looks real to me," she murmured.

"Me, too," Megan agreed with a grin, which she hid behind her teacup.

Shannon lifted her hand and watched the small diamond flash in the sunlight through the window. "The ring is. The engagement isn't," she insisted.

Megan set the cup on its saucer. "His mother's ring. That's very romantic."

Shannon rolled her eyes while Kate laughed in delight. The three cousins had met for lunch at the café later in the week to catch up on each other's happenings. The big news had been the break-ins and the ransacking of the two houses.

"It was a month ago today that the other robbery took place," Kate reminded them. "The night Shannon was shot."

"The twenty-third of December." Shannon smiled ruefully. "I remember it well. You two spent most of Christmas in the hospital with me."

Her throat closed up, and she was overcome by love for her family. "You were there for me," she said huskily, "when I was frightened and couldn't see at all."

Rory, too, had visited and brought her flowers, unlike the attorney—odd, she could hardly recall ever dating Brad—who had disappeared at the first sign of trouble. So much for a man she'd thought was dependable.

"Kate's the one. She's always been there for both of us when we've needed her," Megan said, sadness in her green eyes.

Shannon experienced another wave of fierce love for her cousins. They had shared so much, both sadness and joy.

The hostess seated someone behind them. Shannon's chair was bumped rather forcefully. She glanced over her shoulder and froze, then forced herself to breathe deeply.

"Sorry," the man said, his face hardly more than a foot away from hers as he took his seat and turned to her.

"That's okay." She scooted in closer to the table, her mind in a whirl of disjointed images. The gas station. The robbery. The perpetrator…the man who was seated behind her at this moment!

She could identify that angular face, the scar through the left eyebrow, the thin lips with the snarly smile. She had to tell Rory…no, Jess. And the sheriff.

"Well," she said casually, "that was delicious. Megan, are you ready to go? You were going to help me with grocery shopping."

Megan gave her a surprised glance. "Sure."

After they paid, then said their farewells to Kate on the street, Shannon clutched Megan's arm. "Act like you're leading me. I want to go to Rory's office. We can call Jess from there."

"What is it?"

"Remember the man sitting behind me in the café? He was the one who robbed the store."

"The one who shot you?"

"Yes."

"We need to tell Jess—"

"He'll see us if we go across the street to the sheriff's office, and he'll have time to get away. Rory's office is just down from the grocery."

They hurried off, Shannon holding Megan's arm. Rory met them at the door of his building. "Hi. You ladies had lunch? I just got back from the Herriot place—"

"We've got to call Jess. The perp is in the café," Shannon interrupted.

"The one who shot her," Megan added.

He didn't waste time asking questions but led the way through a side door into his office. He punched in the number, discovered Jess was out and spoke to the sheriff.

"Gene wants to know if you can do a positive ID," Rory said to her.

Shannon nodded. "I can pick him out of a lineup."

"Okay," he said into the phone, listened, said goodbye and hung up. "Let's head over to his office. He'll have the guy in custody by the time we get there."

"Too bad he won't get to finish lunch," Shannon said sincerely. "The trout was wonderful."

Rory burst out laughing. "You," he said, "are too much." Then he kissed her lightly on the mouth.

Piqued, Shannon accompanied him and her grinning cousin to the sheriff's office. After a fifteen-minute wait, Gene asked her to check out the lineup he'd assembled.

"I'll need binoculars," she told him. "Or else I'll have to get in their faces."

With binoculars in hand, she easily identified the man as the perp. He insisted she was confused. "She can't even see," he shouted at the deputy who hand-cuffed him and read him the Miranda.

"She got her sight back. Too bad for you," the sheriff said without a trace of sympathy. "Book him, fingerprint him and lock him up."

The man yelled obscenities at her as they took him away. Rory took hold of her arm. "Good thing he's being locked up. I have an urge to bash his face in."

Gene chuckled. "I'm fighting the same urge. You up to signing a statement?" he asked Shannon.

"Yes," she answered, following Gene to his office to clear up the legalities.

"I'll see you tonight," Rory said later, when he and Shannon and Megan were standing on the sidewalk outside the sheriff's office.

"Tonight?" Shannon tried to remember if she'd agreed to dinner or something.

Although Rory had slept in her guest room for the past four nights, he'd been gone each morning when she awoke. They had shared a cup of cocoa each night when he'd arrived late in the evening, obviously tired.

And each night, she'd had to struggle not to go to him.

If he loved her, if she loved him, how different their lives might have been. If he loved her...

Because she *did* love him. The knowledge flowed through her with the sweet sadness of old dreams long departed. How could she not love him? He was everything she'd ever dreamed of in a man.

"Yes. I'll be in early. Then we'll talk," he added.

After Megan left her at her house, Shannon put her groceries away and wondered what Rory wanted to discuss.

Maybe his folks were leaving and he wanted to break the pretend engagement and get his mother's ring back.

Touching the lovely diamond, she felt a tremendous lowering of her spirits. Love songs and stories had it all wrong. Being in love wasn't exhilarating.

What had the bard said? "A madness most discreet, a choking gall and preserving sweet."

All that and more, she agreed. With a sigh, she went back to work. Clouds gathered over the valley during the long afternoon. More snow was forecast.

At four, the sky was dark and the wind from the mountains was frigid with the promise of bad weather. Rising and turning off the computer, Shannon pulled on her boots and outdoor clothing and went for a walk along the country lane. A crow cawed noisily at her as she crossed the bridge where the creek and road intersected.

The Windraven legacy, she mused. When the wind blew down from the mountain and the ravens cawed at twilight, disaster would follow within twenty-four hours. Usually to someone in her family.

The hair prickled on her nape when another crow joined the first, and they screeched at her for disturbing them. When the snow started falling, the crows fell silent. That seemed even more ominous.

Thirty minutes later, returning to her house, Shannon walked down the driveway to the cable that led to her back door. The shadows of the trees along the creek loomed dark and forbidding around her. The only sounds were those of the snow hitting the crusty drifts of last week and that of the lonely, mournful wind. She felt as if she were the only person in the world.

Rory frowned at the strange car in the driveway, blocking his entrance into the garage. More company?

Just what he needed.

Climbing out of the truck, he stood for a minute in the icy chill of the wind off the mountain and stretched tired muscles. He'd had to put down the Herriot mare that afternoon, a task that was never easy, but had been made harder by the fact that Kyle was his oldest friend. They'd suffered through school from kindergarten to graduation, through deaths of parents—Kyle's dad, his mom—and the loss of first loves...innocence...dreams...

My, but he was feeling morbid tonight. He needed to see Shannon. That always made him feel better.

Needed to?

Yeah.

Retrieving the food he'd brought home for dinner, he went into the house, curious about the owner of the car.

"Rory," his stepmother said. "Come into the living room. You'll never guess who I ran into today in town."

With a sardonic lift of an eyebrow, he left the bags in the kitchen and went down the hall. "Well, hello," he said with a smile. "I *am* surprised."

"Rory," Sandra Wheeler said, rising and coming to him.

They had dated briefly during high school, then she'd dumped him for the new banker's son. Holding no grudges, he returned her embrace warmly.

"What brings you back to these parts?" he asked.

She grimaced. "Divorce."

"Hey, I'm sorry."

"Don't be. I'm not. Ten years was more than enough to get over my illusions about marriage and fidelity. Luckily, we both agreed that we didn't want children too soon, so we don't have that complication."

He nodded, recalling his own words about marriage and fidelity, spoken to Shannon not long ago. His chest did the usual funny little pang under the breastbone when he thought of her.

"Can you stay for dinner?" he asked. "I brought some stuff home—"

"I thought we would go out," his stepmother broke in. "The four of us. I want to hear all about your family," she said to Sandra. "Your mother and I were friends in high school. Of course, that was back in the Dark Ages to you young people."

While everyone laughed, Rory gave his stepmom a quick study. What was she up to now? The woman was conniving, and he could spot trouble from a mile off.

Feeling uneasy, he told his guest to make herself at home. "I brought something for dinner. There's enough for everyone. I'll run next door and get Shannon."

"Shannon?" Sandra said with a glance at Catherine.

"My fiancée," he told her and noted the flicker of surprise in her gorgeous blue eyes. His stepmother had evidently forgotten to mention that detail. "Be right back."

The light was on in the kitchen when he crossed

the yard to Shannon's house. He found her there, dressed in gray slacks and a blue sweater, a blue and gray scarf tied around her throat.

"Hi, beautiful," he said, his voice going thick with the desire he couldn't suppress when he was with her.

Shannon's heart melted at his smile and the warmth in his eyes. "Hi, yourself."

Then she sort of dived into his arms, eager for his touch and the fire of his kiss. She wasn't disappointed. His mouth closed over hers with the hungry tenderness she'd come to expect from him.

"Ready for dinner?" he asked when they came up for air.

"I'd rather stay here," she said impulsively, then felt her face flame as the words gave her innermost feelings away. She stared up at him anxiously, not certain how to retract the admission.

"Me, too," he murmured. "More than you can possibly know." He opened the door. "But we have guests to tend to."

His tone held an undercurrent she couldn't decipher. Worried, she walked with him across the yard and bridge to his house. There she spoke to his parents and to a new person, an "old school friend," as his stepmother put it.

"Sandra and Rory were a couple long ago. I believe she was his first love," Catherine confided to Shannon after the introductions.

"Actually, Shannon's cousin Kate was my first love," Rory corrected. "She picked me up after I fell off the jungle gym. I was in kindergarten and she was in first grade. An older woman," he added with a wicked grin.

As the evening wore on, it became clear that Catherine had chosen her old friend's daughter for her stepson and that the daughter was interested. Shannon found herself with less and less to say. Finally, as the other two woman dominated the conversation, she fell silent.

At nine, she rose. "If you'll excuse me. No, don't get up. I can make it without help," she told Rory.

"I'll walk you home," he said firmly.

But while he retrieved his jacket and said goodnight to his guest, she slipped out the back door. Grabbing the cable because the night was very dark due to the clouds, she ran toward her house and the safety of being alone with her emotions. She was very near tears for no reason she could determine, except she felt unbearably tired and everything seemed too much all at once.

"Shannon," a male voice called out just as she stepped up on the little porch.

Without looking around, she rushed into the house and slammed the door as if, by doing so, she could hide from him. When he knocked, she stepped back.

He entered and closed the door behind him, then gave the dead bolt a flick, locking them in.

Shannon removed her outerwear and insulated boots. "I, uh, I'm tired."

"What are you thinking?" he asked, ignoring her attempt to get him to leave. He tossed his jacket on top of hers on the hook beside the door.

"Nothing. I had a nice evening." She paused. "Your friend is very attractive—"

"That has nothing to do with me." He gave her a stern frown. "There's nothing my stepmother, or anyone else, can do to interfere with us, provided we don't let them. Do you understand?"

She nodded, then, hesitantly, shook her head.

He laughed briefly, ruefully. "Catherine has decided she's the perfect mother and I'm the ungrateful stepchild. She declared she's looking out after my interests. I disagreed. In fact, I told her to butt out. I'll extend to her the courtesy due my father's wife, but that's the only relationship we'll ever have. I think I got that point across, thanks to you."

"Me?" she said, astounded.

"My stepmother now understands that I'm very much in love with my fiancée, that there's room for only one woman in my heart because she fills it completely."

Shannon was aghast. "You told her that?"

"Yes."

"What about your guest?"

"Since she was in the room while Catherine and I held our discussion, I'm sure she understands, too. I really don't know. Or care."

Suddenly he was very close. Shannon backed up a step. He followed and laid his hands on the counter on each side of her, trapping her within his warmth. She stared up at him in confusion. His eyes—those beautiful eyes—were sending her messages, but she wasn't sure she was reading them right.

Her heart leaped around in her chest and landed in her throat. She swallowed hard, the hated uncertainty rising in her along with the longing to lay her head on his chest and let the world fade away. She knew that wasn't possible.

"You're the hardest female to read I've ever met," he complained softly. "I wonder about you and your feelings. Give me a clue, lady cop. I need one desperately."

"What do you mean?"

He leaned over her, his lips dangerously close. She wanted to throw her arms around him, to cling to him, to demand that he love her...

She dropped her head forward, her forehead against his chest, so he wouldn't see the longing in her eyes. Love was the most confusing thing she'd ever felt. With an effort, she willed the harsh burn of impending tears away.

"I mean," he whispered in a tone that sent waves of longing crashing through her, "do you think you could care enough to continue the engagement?"

She stared up at him. Two tears escaped and slipped down her face, burning a trail straight to her heart. He caught them on his finger.

"Give me a chance to make you fall in love with me."

The air thickened. Her lungs flatly refused to breathe. She became light-headed.

After a second, he stepped back. A resigned smile flickered over his finely chiseled mouth. "No, huh?"

He reached for his coat while she stood there like a post, unable to move.

"Ironic, isn't it?" he continued. "To meet the one woman I've dreamed of and not be able to win her. As they say—that's life."

He reached for the door. She caught his arm. "What woman?" she asked, suddenly able to breathe again. "What dream? What are you saying?"

His glance flicked from her hand to her face. He studied her for a minute. "This woman."

He touched her chin with a finger.

"This dream."

He took her hand and laid it against his heart.

"Please. Be specific."

"All right." He laid both hands on her shoulders and pulled her near so she could see his face clearly. "You're that woman. The dream is you. I've fallen for you. Hard. Now you can laugh."

She shook her head. Placing both hands against his chest, she whispered, "How can I laugh at my guardian angel, my Good Samaritan, who gave me life when I thought it was gone?"

His grip tightened. "Dammit, I don't want gratitude. I want..." He took a deep breath. "I want your love. I want your future. I want...you, just you."

He felt sweat gathering on his upper lip, along his spine and his scalp, as he waited for her answer. He'd never realized how scary love could be, how it felt to lay your heart bare before another and wait for them to scoop it up and tuck it safely away...or to trample on it.

It was all up to this woman. *If she loved him…as he loved her.*

He saw the hesitation in her eyes and knew she was thinking of the future. Proud, independent little cuss.

His heart melted into a soft blob as he waited, knowing she had to come to him freely or else reject his love and turn away from all the wild, sweet possibilities of a future between them.

"Are you saying you love me?" she asked.

He was surprised by the question. "Of course. Why else would I want to tie myself to a former cop who's studied psychology and will probably analyze every move I make for the rest of my life?"

She frowned at him, but he relaxed. There was laughter in her eyes. A smile lurked at the corners of her mouth. She touched his face and explored it with both hands, running her fingertips along his jaw and up to his temples as she'd done before, as if she would know him through touch rather than sight, as if she could read his soul through the simple contact. He hoped she could.

"I love you, lady cop," he said and closed his eyes because it meant too much, *she* meant too much.

"I love you, too," Shannon said, suddenly understanding that the confession was difficult for him, too, that he, too, was vulnerable. "I was afraid, but I couldn't seem to stop it. I thought you felt responsible for me—"

His eyes snapped open. With a whoop, he lifted her off the floor and swung her around, then plopped her on the counter before she had time to think. His smile dazzled her heart.

"I do feel responsible," he said, nuzzling her cheek. "Because I want to be. I want to make you so happy you won't remember what life was like before we met."

"Then hold me," she said. "Always."

He caught her face between his hands, his touch gentle, and pressed a thousand kisses on her eager mouth. The flames crackled between them and threatened to get out of control.

From the road, they heard the sound of a car leaving. In a minute, his old flame was gone. Shannon took a deep breath and let it go along with the uncertainty. Nothing and no one could interfere with their love, she realized.

His gaze devoured her. Little shivers of delight danced over her skin each time she met his eyes. They laughed for no reason at all...and kissed for all the reasons in the world. They talked about the future.

Later, going to his house, Shannon forced herself to be calm and try to appear rational. Which was difficult with her head filled with the wonder of being in love. It was hard for him, too, she saw, meeting his lambent gaze as they entered his kitchen.

His stepmother was at the stove. "I've made coffee."

"Thank you." Shannon said. "That was thoughtful."

The other woman looked from her to Rory. Her eyes met Shannon's. She smiled suddenly.

''So he really has fallen in love,'' she said as if she found this news very satisfying. ''Good. His father and I were worried about his future. Now we can relax.''

Rory glanced at Shannon and gave a slight shrug. She smiled. His stepmother had accepted her in his life. If she ever forgot, well, a wife would be an effective reminder that a person couldn't always direct the world as she thought it should go.

She thought of all her own plans for the future. One thing she'd forgotten to take into account. Love. It had its own agenda.

''When shall we plan to attend the wedding?'' Mr. Daniels asked, entering the room, a calendar in hand.

She and Rory studied the dates. ''Next week?'' her groom suggested, his manner gratifyingly eager.

''Next month? Catherine and Kate have to help me plan it,'' Shannon said, including her soon-to-be step-mother-in-law in the planning. ''Megan will be my maid of honor.'' She glanced at Rory. ''Who's to be the best man?''

''Kyle Herriot.''

She'd known the two men were friends, but there was still a lot to be learned about her love. Odd, to know someone all her life and realize how little she had known the inner person.

As if reading her thoughts, Rory leaned close. ''We'll have the rest of our lives to learn all about each other. We already know the most important things.''

She tilted her head and gave him a saucy smile. "Such as?"

"Courage. Integrity. Respect. Loyalty. Love."

"I think that sums it up."

Later, when they were alone at her house, after they'd called Kate and Megan and explained everything, he built a fire in the grate in the living room. They settled on the sofa, her secure in his arms.

"I really don't understand love at all," she told him honestly. "I've looked through my books on relationships and nothing truly explains it...not the wonder of it."

Rory read between the lines and saw her concerns. "Or what makes it last for some people and not for others."

"Yes."

"I think each person has to make the commitment in his or her own heart. Each time that commitment is threatened, when things get hard, or dull, or whatever, then they have to decide to make the commitment again...and again."

"And they should let the other person know they're still serious about making it work," she added.

He smiled at her, the awful, achy tenderness rushing through him in a tidal wave of lust and love and all the other things that went into a relationship. "We can do that," he assured her.

"Let's always be honest with each other about how we feel and what we need from each other, even if it hurts at times."

"Always," he vowed. "You know, I never wanted

to make promises before. Now I find it's easy. With you, it is. I want to promise you the moon and the stars and everything you want."

"That's easy, too. You're what I want. You and two kids and a dog," she added, happiness overflowing her heart.

"Two cats. And some 4-H calves."

"An Olympic champion jumper from the famous Windraven stables," she added, recalling his dream. "You will name your line after the ranch, won't you?"

"If that's what you want."

She kissed him, then realized plans for the future weren't the only thing she wanted. "You," she whispered. "I want you. Now."

He gathered her close, then stretched out on the sofa, their hearts beating as one. "You got me, lady cop. From the day I noticed you walking across the street with a bunch of kids following along behind like the Pied Piper's band. It was ordained from that moment."

She blinked in confusion. "But that was before Christmas."

"Yeah. I don't know what took me so long. You were right here under my nose all the time."

She couldn't help but laugh. "Lucky for us that I got shot in the head and you found me, huh?"

"Yeah, lucky," he repeated.

Gazing into his eyes, she felt his love reach right down to her toes. For a second, she considered a future in which her sight went away, then realized it wasn't so scary anymore. Rory was a man who stuck by his promises. She sighed as her heart started its familiar thumping and raised her face for his kiss.

Sometimes a person just had to accept things on faith without fully understanding it. Like male-female attraction. Like love.

"I love you," he murmured. "Don't ever doubt it."

"I won't. I love you," she told him. "Don't ever forget it."

"Never," he said. "And that's a promise."

And so it was. She realized the safest love was that which was fully felt and returned by the other person. With this man, she had found her heart's haven.

"My love," she whispered as they shared laughter and passion and all the other things that were part of the most precious gift of all.

*　*　*　*　*

Beloved author
Sherryl Woods
is back with a brand-new miniseries

THE CALAMITY JANES

Five women. Five Dreams.
A lifetime of friendship....

On Sale May 2001—DO YOU TAKE THIS REBEL?
Silhouette Special Edition

On Sale August 2001—COURTING THE ENEMY
Silhouette Special Edition

On Sale September 2001—TO CATCH A THIEF
Silhouette Special Edition

On Sale October 2001—THE CALAMITY JANES
Silhouette Single Title

On Sale November 2001—WRANGLING THE REDHEAD
Silhouette Special Edition

"Sherryl Woods is an author who writes with
a very special warmth, wit, charm and intelligence."
—*New York Times* bestselling author
Heather Graham Pozzessere

Available at your favorite retail outlet.

Silhouette®
TM
Where love comes alive™

Visit Silhouette at www.eHarlequin.com   SSETCJR

SILHOUETTE®
MAKES YOU
A STAR!

Feel like a star with Silhouette.

We will fly you and a guest to New York City for an
exciting weekend stay at a glamorous 5-star hotel.
Experience a refreshing day at one of New York's
trendiest spas and have your photo taken by a
professional. Plus, receive $1,000 U.S. spending money!

Flowers...long walks...dinner for two... how does Silhouette Books make romance come alive for you?

Send us a script, with 500 words or less, along with visuals (only drawings,
magazine cutouts or photographs or combination thereof). Show us how
Silhouette Makes Your Love Come Alive. Be creative and have fun. No
purchase necessary. All entries must be clearly marked with your name,
address and telephone number. All entries will become property of
Silhouette and are not returnable. **Contest closes September 28, 2001.**

Please send your entry to: **Silhouette Makes You a Star!**

In U.S.A.	In Canada
P.O. Box 9069	P.O. Box 637
Buffalo, NY, 14269-9069	Fort Erie, ON, L2A 5X3

Look for contest details on the next page, by visiting www.eHarlequin.com or
request a copy by sending a self-addressed envelope to the applicable address
above. Contest open to Canadian and U.S. residents who are 18 or over.
Void where prohibited.

Silhouette®

Where love comes alive™

Our lucky winner's photo will appear in a Silhouette ad. Join the fun!

SRMYAS1

HARLEQUIN "SILHOUETTE MAKES YOU A STAR!" CONTEST 1308
OFFICIAL RULES
NO PURCHASE NECESSARY TO ENTER

1. To enter, follow directions published in the offer to which you are responding. Contest begins June 1, 2001, and ends on September 28, 2001. Entries must be postmarked by September 28, 2001, and received by October 5, 2001. Enter by hand-printing (or typing) on an 8 ½" x 11" piece of paper your name, address (including zip code), contest number/name and attaching a script containing <u>500 words or less, along with drawings, photographs or magazine cutouts, or combinations thereof</u> (i.e., collage) <u>on no larger than 9" x 12"</u> piece of paper, describing how the <u>Silhouette books make romance come alive for you.</u> Mail via first-class mail to: Harlequin "Silhouette Makes You a Star!" Contest 1308, (in the U.S.) P.O. Box 9069, Buffalo, NY 14269-9069, (in Canada) P.O. Box 637, Fort Erie, Ontario, Canada L2A 5X3. Limit one entry per person, household or organization.

2. Contests will be judged by a panel of members of the Harlequin editorial, marketing and public relations staff. Fifty percent of criteria will be judged against script and fifty percent will be judged against drawing, photographs and/or magazine cutouts. Judging criteria will be based on the following:

   • Sincerity—25%
   • Originality and Creativity—50%
   • Emotionally Compelling—25%

   In the event of a tie, duplicate prizes will be awarded. Decisions of the judges are final.

3. All entries become the property of Torstar Corp. and may be used for future promotional purposes. Entries will not be returned. No responsibility is assumed for lost, late, illegible, incomplete, inaccurate, nondelivered or misdirected mail.

4. Contest open only to residents of the U.S. <u>(except Puerto Rico)</u> and Canada who are 18 years of age or older, and is void wherever prohibited by law; all applicable laws and regulations apply. Any litigation within the Province of Quebec respecting the conduct or organization of a publicity contest may be submitted to the Régie des alcools, des courses et des jeux for a ruling. Any litigation respecting the awarding of a prize may be submitted to the Régie des alcools, des courses et des jeux only for the purpose of helping the parties reach a settlement. Employees and immediate family members of Torstar Corp. and D. L. Blair, Inc., their affiliates, subsidiaries and all other agencies, entities and persons connected with the use, marketing or conduct of this contest are not eligible to enter. Taxes on prizes are the sole responsibility of the winner. Acceptance of any prize offered constitutes permission to use winner's name, photograph or other likeness for the purposes of advertising, trade and promotion on behalf of Torstar Corp., its affiliates and subsidiaries without further compensation to the winner, unless prohibited by law.

5. Winner will be determined no later than November 30, 2001, and will be notified by mail. Winner will be required to sign and return an Affidavit of Eligibility/Release of Liability/Publicity Release form within 15 days after winner notification. Noncompliance within that time period may result in disqualification and an alternative winner may be selected. All travelers must execute a Release of Liability prior to ticketing and must possess required travel documents (e.g., passport, photo ID) where applicable. Trip must be booked by December 31, 2001, and completed within one year of notification. No substitution of prize permitted by winner. Torstar Corp. and D. L. Blair, Inc., their parents, affiliates and subsidiaries are not responsible for errors in printing of contest, entries and/or game pieces. In the event of printing or other errors that may result in unintended prize values or duplication of prizes, all affected game pieces or entries shall be null and void. **Purchase or acceptance of a product offer does not improve your chances of winning.**

6. Prizes: (1) Grand Prize—A 2-night/3-day trip for two (2) to New York City, including round-trip coach air transportation nearest winner's home and hotel accommodations (double occupancy) at The Plaza Hotel, a glamorous afternoon makeover at <u>a trendy New York spa</u>, $1,000 in U.S. spending money and an opportunity to <u>have a professional photo taken and appear in a Silhouette advertisement</u> (approximate retail value: $7,000). (10) Ten Runner-Up Prizes of gift packages (retail value $50 ea.). Prizes consist of only those items listed as part of the prize. Limit one prize per person. Prize is valued in U.S. currency.

7. For the name of the winner (available after December 31, 2001) send a self-addressed, stamped envelope to: Harlequin "Silhouette Makes You a Star!" Contest 1197 Winners, P.O. Box 4200 Blair, NE 68009-4200 or you may access the www.eHarlequin.com Web site through February 28, 2002.

Contest sponsored by Torstar Corp., P.O Box 9042, Buffalo, NY 14269-9042.

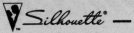